MW00975402

John Bittleston

Illustrations by Lee Kowling

SINGLETON PTE LTD

© 1992 Singleton Pte Ltd

Published by: Singleton Pte Ltd
No 1 Shenton Way
#19-04 Robina House
Singapore 0106

Designed by: Kelly Chopard
Typeset & Printed by: Letraprint

ISBN 981-00-3903-4

All rights reserved. No part of this publication may be reproduced or transmitted in any form or by any means, electronic, mechanical, including photocopy, recording, or any information storage and retrieval system without permission in writing from the publisher.

For Eliza,

dedicated researcher and dearest friend

INTRODUCTION

Wiglington and Wenks are two Water Rats who live in a small village in Hampshire, England. In ***The Legacy*** they discovered that Wiglington is related to a very famous map-maker who travelled with Marco Polo.

Carto Wiglington made many maps but left them, for safety, in the places where he drew them. Unfortunately, he was swept away in a storm without having collected his maps together and nobody has come forward in the seven hundred years since then to claim them.

As a result the valuable maps have been hidden away. Wiglington and Wenks are determined to find the maps so that they can be put on display and the money collected from exhibiting them can be used to set up a Trust for cartography students.

There is a remote branch of the family who are Fruit Bats, headed by Fruba. They will go to almost any length to get hold of the maps first, so that they can sell them for a lot of money and repair the belfries in which they live, most of which are in a disastrous state.

Wiglington and Wenks discovered the first map, with the help of their friend Castle, in the archives of the Louvre in Paris. Even though their conversations were bugged and they were attacked by the Batpack they won through. This was because they had the help of SecuriRat whose Chief Officer, Mr Ruthless, saw to it that they were not harmed.

Following an exciting chase, they managed to bring the map to the British Museum where their friend, Sir Ordy Nance, was waiting to put it safely in the vault.

In *The Chase* they visited Venice, the Water Rat Centre of the World, where they met The Genius who helped them unravel the clues to where the next maps could be found. This led them to Rome and a visit to a Very Important Person. Their efforts were rewarded and they brought several of Carto Wiglington's maps home.

In *The Crossroads* they go to Turkey in pursuit of more Carto Wiglington maps. Zeki, a well-known guide, befriended them in Istanbul and managed to help them in their quest while at the same time showing them something of the city. The search took them to Ephesus, Izmir, Bodrum and Pamukkale. They were successful and swelled the numbers of maps brought back to England.

A new menace had appeared on the scene in the form of the Huntergrunden. This meant that they must make haste to continue to trace their heritage.

CHAPTER 1

BEWARE THE HUNTERGRUNDEN

Wiglington and Wenks had just finished breakfast. During the summer they often took their first meal of the day outside. In the early morning it was warm but not too hot and the fresh smell of the flowers and the ripening corn gave them a hearty appetite.

Neither of them moved. The urgency to plan another visit was not such that it should disturb the period after meals when they chatted about things. It was their favourite time and they let nothing interfere with it.

Well, almost nothing. Even as they sat there the telephone rang and Wiglington went inside the house to answer it. A few minutes later he returned, looking pale.

"That was Mr Ruthless of SecuriRat," he announced, "he says he has important matters to discuss with us. He will be here within the hour."

What Mr Ruthless had to say was indeed serious.

"You will recall," he began, his hands clutching his bright red braces as if for support, "you will recall that Fruba told you about his experience with the Huntergrunden when he was carrying the fake maps back from Turkey. Mention was made of a certain Count Cannaregio whom you had met in Venice. In fact, I think you dined with him, didn't you?"

Wiglington and Wenks nodded.

"I'm afraid that what Fruba was saying has turned out to be the truth. The Huntergrunden are a much-feared gang operating internationally but with their most powerful forces at work in the

The Huntergrunden are a much-feared gang operating internationally but with their most powerful forces at work in the Mediterranean.

Mediterranean. They are an unusual group because they are a combination of humans like Count Cannaregio and animals, mostly wolves. These are not your gentle wolves like Sheba whom you met in Izmir, but rough and dangerous creatures, killers if necessary. They have recruited CorporalBat and a small number of dissident Bats who have absconded from the original Batpack."

Mr Ruthless paused to let his words sink in and to take a sip of the excellent tea Wenks had brought him.

"Are they more troublesome than the Batpack were when they were against us?" asked Wenks, concerned that they might find themselves having battles like the ones they had had rescuing the maps from Paris and Rome.

"I'm very much afraid they are," replied Mr Ruthless, continuing, "you see, they already have a Carto Wiglington map, we believe. That puts them in a position where not only do they have an incentive to obtain more maps but they may also have a clue about where others are. Don't forget that each map is supposed to provide enough information to find the next one, if only you know where to look for it."

"Of which country is the map that they already have?" enquired Wenks.

"We don't know that at present," replied Mr Ruthless, "the fact that it is valuable was most likely brought to their attention by your appearance in Venice."

"So what do you recommend that we do?" asked Wiglington.

"It is vital that we warn Sir Ordy without delay," replied Mr Ruthless stirring his tea vigorously, "because our information suggests that the Huntergrunden may even be planning an attack on the British Museum. Of course they wouldn't do anything like trying to break into the vault where the maps are but they are not above setting up an inside job. Remember they have Count Cannaregio who provides a good deal of influence should they need it."

"Well, it's easy to warn Sir Ordy," said Wiglington, "not so easy for him to take action that will guarantee the safety of the maps, however. But beyond warning him, what other action should we take?"

"The decision is yours, of course," replied Mr Ruthless, "but I think you should pursue the next map in Malta where the Huntergrunden have their headquarters. The objective should be to find and retrieve the map, if they do have one, and seek the remaining ones as quickly as possible. Otherwise they may capture more maps and get ahead on the trail leaving you behind."

The matter was clearly one of considerable urgency and Wiglington and Wenks arranged an early meeting with Sir Ordy Nance at the British Museum. His help in finding, identifying and safeguarding the maps so far had been invaluable. Now it was time for him to guide their next moves in the face of the new enemy and the dangers they posed.

Sir Ordy supported Mr Ruthless. Wiglington and Wenks should proceed without delay to Malta and deal with the Huntergrunden on their own ground.

The news that the Huntergrunden were thinking of attacking the British Museum was also serious.

"Of course," Sir Ordy told them, "the British Museum is a haven of safety from any form of outside attack. But all organisations, including this one, are vulnerable to 'inside jobs'. I take the matter so seriously that I think I shall have to stay here and miss a visit to Malta, much as I would like to have accompanied you."

"I don't want to alarm you unnecessarily but you should understand that in the Huntergrunden you have an adversary of a completely different sort from the Batpack. Oh, the Fruit Bats can be tiresome," he laughed, "and their batdroppings can cause a lot of damage. But the Huntergrunden are cunning and, if you'll pardon the expression, ruthless." He bowed in the direction of Mr Ruthless who grinned.

"My dears," he went on, "this is such a vital matter that it should be mentioned at the *Very Top*." What the *Very Top* meant wasn't clear to Wiglington and Wenks. Mr Ruthless, however, nodded in agreement and tapped the side of his nose knowingly, so they assumed it was the right thing to do.

Wiglington and Wenks continued to wonder what *Very Top* meant as they travelled home later that afternoon.

Sir Ordy appeared in Bentley two days later, accompanied by Mr Ruthless.

"I have spoken to the *Very Top*," he said, "and the matter is regarded as one for Major Consideration." He sat back with a satisfied look on his face.

Frankly, Wiglington and Wenks had no idea who this apparently military gentleman, Major Consideration, was, but if he was going to help find and preserve the Carto Wiglington maps, they were all for it.

Sir Ordy and Mr Ruthless seemed very pleased with what they had done and even accepted a glass of mulberry wine before departing once again for London. They promised to return when the matter had been given major consideration.

Meanwhile, of course, Wiglington and Wenks were under constant surveillance by RatGuard. He, or one of his colleagues, was on duty twenty-four hours a day.

Their search for further maps was to be helped more than they could possibly have expected. When Sir Ordy and Mr Ruthless returned a few days later they were positively glowing.

"I am happy to tell you," said Sir Ordy, "that Major Consideration has resulted in the Government classifying the matter as of National Importance. It fears there could be an International Incident if it is not handled properly. Clearly, it would no longer be safe for you to travel in the Ratbag vehicle made for you by the Batpack. Much too vulnerable and exposed, not to mention visible. So the Government has decided to assign you a small submarine which will act as your transport, your accommodation and your fortress for the coming expedition. It will travel underwater for much of the time and will have a specially trained crew capable of dealing with an enemy without having to go to war."

Sir Ordy paused for breath.

"How very considerate," said Wiglington, "Wenks, we shall enjoy living in a submarine for a time, shan't we?"

"I'm sure I don't know," replied Wenks, "I've never been in a submarine before. Will it be very hot?"

Mr Ruthless laughed.

"Oh no," he said, "even old submarines are now fully air-conditioned. The temperature inside the vessel will be constant. The only thing you may find is that it is rather small. But," he looked them up and down, "that really shouldn't pose a problem for you two."

"It would be polite of us to write a thank-you note to Major Consideration, wouldn't it?" enquired Wenks, adding, "where should we address it?"

"It's a very good idea," replied Sir Ordy, "just put '10, Downing Street, London' on it. That will make sure it gets there."

It must have been the only letter ever to arrive at Downing St which began "Dear Major".

There were lots of questions to be asked. What sort of clothes do you need for a submarine? Should they take their own rations or would food be provided? Did they need to practise sleeping in a hammock?

"It would be polite of us to write a thank-you note for Major Consideration, wouldn't it?" enquired Wenks.

Sir Ordy and Mr Ruthless could answer some of them but they told Wiglington and Wenks to keep most of the questions for their visit to Portsmouth the following week when they would look over the submarine allotted to them and meet the Captain and the crew.

It was a time of great preparation for them. The prospect of being in the charge of the Royal Navy plus the fact that they were going to be travelling below water made them exuberant and not a little nervous. They went into their local market town and bought thick navy pullovers and warm knitted hats with tassels.

"You never know when we may surface," said Wiglington who had been reading about submarines, "and it could be very cold on the conning tower."

"What's the 'conning tower'?" asked Wenks.

"You'll see when we get there," replied Wiglington remembering that they were in a public place and he should be careful of what he said. You didn't know who might be listening.

There were other preparations to be made as well. Mr Ruthless had suggested that the Ratbag should be sent to Malta independently. He felt it might come in handy on the spot. After all, a submarine can't go everywhere and they would be sure to need transport on the island.

That night they didn't sleep much. Partly, it was all the excitement that kept them awake. Partly, it was the activity around the house. It seemed that RatGuard had called for reinforcements for some reason. Anyway, there were lots of sentries with torches scurrying this way and that and they even saw the flashing blue light of a police car reflected on the bedroom ceiling at one point. RatGuard had warned them about increased comings and goings and told them it was routine and they should just stay indoors and take no notice. Which was easier said than done.

But partly they lay awake that night because of the distant baying of what sounded awfully like a pack of wolves.

CHAPTER 2

HMS REPELLER

The worst hours if you can't sleep are usually those just before dawn. Your body slows down then and you often feel quite low. Fortunately, the mood passes with dawn and thc joy of sunrise lifts the spirit and brings hope with the new day.

Wiglington and Wenks had such a bad night that they got up in the early hours and made themselves cocoa. If made very sweet and very strong it often puts people to sleep.

So Wiglington and Wenks fell asleep just as the day was beginning and didn't wake up until the sun was well in the sky.

"My goodness!" exclaimed Wiglington, "whatever is the time?"

Fortunately it wasn't too late and they made up for oversleeping by hurrying and having a very quick breakfast. The navy car arrived just as they had finished.

"Good morning, Sir, M'am," said the smart young sailor as he opened the door. Wiglington and Wenks felt very grand being whisked away at great speed to Portsmouth.

RatGuard had bustled them rather hurriedly from their home to the car and they had only managed to glimpse the changes that had taken place since they went indoors the day before. Obviously, all the noise they had heard during the night was about putting barricades in place. There was a good deal of barbed wire, and large lights had been set up to illuminate the surroundings of the barn — presumably in case of intruders.

"If we're not careful," said Wiglington, "it'll look like a battleground."

"In a sense, I suppose that's what it has become," replied Wenks, adding, "though I'd rather it didn't. Bentley was such a nice, quiet place until first the Batpack and then the Huntergrunden got involved."

The car sped on, the driver speaking only occasionally, usually to point out some object of naval interest. Soon they reached Portsmouth and were taken straight to the Submarine Museum to be given a briefing on the history and technology of this particular form of naval achievement.

A marvellous man called Gus showed them around. He had been a submariner himself and since his retirement he had been a leading light at the Museum. He was a very knowledgeable man.

When they had had a tour with explanations which, quite honestly, they only barely understood, they were taken to meet the Commander of HMS Repeller. She was not a new submarine. The age of nuclear power had not reached back that far. Nor was she a large submarine, by today's standards.

But to Wiglington and Wenks she was the most beautiful ship in the world. Her long, sleek body looked like an arrow set to pierce the water. Her conning tower, which Wenks now understood, was stately and majestic. At rest on the surface, she looked the perfect lady. At speed, underwater she must, they thought, have looked a deadly killer.

"How d'you do, Wiglington?" said the Commander, shaking Wiglington vigorously by the paw.

"Welcome aboard, M'am," he said to Wenks, bowing to her as a sign of courtesy, "we're proud to be able to be of assistance in recovering the famous Carto Wiglington maps. My Number One here, Mr Bellows, will show you round while I attend to the matters of readying the ship for departure. After you've seen around and looked at your quarters I hope you will join me and the other officers for a bite of lunch? Jolly good."

He handed them over to the First Officer.

"If you're Number One," asked Wenks, "then what is the Commander? Number Zero?"

Mr Bellows laughed.

A marvellous man called Gus showed them around.

"No," he said, "he's the boss and I'm the next boss. I guess it does sound odd now you mention it. I ought to be called the Number Two, really."

"Well, I'm sure we wouldn't want to demote you," said Wenks, hoping that she hadn't upset the whole tradition of the Navy. She knew there were some peculiar practices but she was sure they had a purpose.

"Drink the Queen's health sitting down, don't you?" enquired Wiglington to show that he knew a few of those practices himself.

"I'll show you why," replied Mr Bellows, leading them to a small dining room. He pointed out the height of the ceiling.

"In Admiral Lord Nelson's day the ceilings were even lower," he said, "and if you were to stand up in a hurry you'd knock yourself out. So the Monarch gave permission for sailors to drink the Loyal Toast sitting down."

Their quarters were splendid. They thought it must have been the best cabin on the ship.

"I hope we didn't displace anyone to get this excellent room," said Wenks, wondering if the First Officer had been turned out for them.

"As a matter of fact," Mr Bellows said, "I shouldn't really tell you this but if you promise not to say anything. . . ."

Wiglington and Wenks nodded.

"This was a special stateroom in case we needed to carry royalty. At the time of the Second World War it was thought that we might have to evacuate the King and Queen. So this submarine was made ready to do so. Of course, it was never used. They would probably have refused to go anyway," he added, "they were not ones for running away from danger."

The Commander introduced them to the other officers before lunch. They were a jolly bunch of sailors, several with full beards.

"Shaving can be a problem in a submarine," observed the Engineer Officer, "especially if we are submerged for a long time."

"Will we feel odd when the submarine is sinking?" asked Wenks.

"Well, we don't like to call it sinking," replied the First Officer, "we refer to it as diving. Sinking sounds so final. And to answer your question, no, you won't feel odd. If you've been up in an aircraft you will have experienced the descent before landing. Diving is much the same as that."

Wiglington and Wenks explained that not only had they flown in a conventional aircraft but they had had their own special plane, the Ratbag. The officers were greatly impressed and not a little amused. They reckoned that the next few weeks were going to be most entertaining and certainly something very different from their normal duty.

When they returned from the dockyard to Bentley their home looked even more like a fortress. Big arc lamps had been set up to light the garden and the surrounding land and the lane. Mr Crosstik and his son had been pressed into service and were working hard to secure the barn and Wiglington and Wenks' home from they knew not what. In fact, they hadn't known that Wiglington and Wenks lived there, nor that they were so important and famous. The farmer who owned the barn gave the helpers his very best cider and an extra glass to Mr Crosstik.

At night they were not allowed to go out. There were sounds of prowlers not far away from the barn and the baying they had heard the night before their visit to HMS Repeller was repeated, though it never seemed to come nearer. No doubt the guards kept whatever it was away.

RatGuard had another senior member of SecuriRat assigned to take turns with him. She was called Miss Protectorat and she was kind and gentle until roused when she was reputed to have a karate chop that could flatten the largest foe.

Wiglington asked if they might take a walk through the village before they were due to depart. At first RatGuard said no. He had strict instructions to avoid letting them be exposed to any risk. But Wenks pleaded.

"It will be such a long time before we can walk through the countryside again and we are going to be cooped up in a submarine all the way to Malta."

"Very well," said RatGuard, relenting, "but we shall have to accompany you and I want an armoured car to follow us just in case."

The little procession set off round the village and all the cottagers peered through their curtains and wondered why Wiglington and Wenks had such an escort.

Two days later the message came that HMS Repeller was ready for boarding and the navy car arrived to collect them.

That night, after the sun had gone down, and when Wiglington and Wenks were tucked up in their bunks, the submarine slipped her moorings and stole silently out of harbour en route to the Mediterranean. There was no moon and as the ship was black the Commander felt it was not necessary to travel submerged. The steady hum of the engines and the gentle *whooshing* of the water alongside the craft were very conducive to sleep. There was no baying of wolves to be heard.

Wiglington and Wenks slept soundly as they were carried by Her Majesty's Navy to their next adventure.

CHAPTER 3

THE SEA WOLVES

The next morning Wiglington and Wenks appeared in their sailor suits. Everyone admired them enormously. The Commander asked them if they would like to go up into the conning tower as it was very calm and he had seen nothing to make him think they should dive.

Climbing up the steep ladder into the hatch that led to the deck was quite difficult. The ladder had been designed with long sailors' legs in mind. But they managed with a little help.

Bollard, the sailor in charge, was a kindly, heavily built sailor with some fifteen years experience of submarines. He had seen service in many parts of the world and had acquired that philosophical approach to life where nothing is too upsetting and everything is taken as it comes. In a tight corner he could move with a speed and precision not immediately apparent from his somewhat plodding approach when things were running smoothly.

His broad, open smile and his willingness to lend a hand to even the most junior recruit made him universally popular with both the sailors and the officers. "I'd trust him with my wallet on a night out in Newcastle," the Commander had been heard to say, giving Bollard the ultimate accolade for honesty.

On the way up Bollard showed them how the escape hatch opened to let people into the conning tower in case of emergency.

"Not that we're likely to have one," he said, "I've never been in an emergency on a submarine in all my years in the Navy. My friend Mallard knew someone who had had to escape from a submerged sub, but it's very rare. We keep in practice, though, just in case."

On deck it was distinctly breezy . . . .

On deck it was distinctly breezy and they were glad of their hats. The Repeller was going at full speed which was about the same speed as the Ratbag. She would be slower under water, the sailor explained.

"So would the Ratbag," said Wiglington, grinning.

After breakfast they were taken to the engine room. The noise was terrific and Wiglington and Wenks had to try to remember all their questions. There was no way they were going to be able to ask them over the din of the engines.

The workings of a submarine, even an old one like the Repeller, are highly complicated and the best explanation in the world wasn't going to tell them much. But they took an interest and learnt some of the terms which they had never heard before.

All about them the sea was quiet and the voyage proceeded smoothly until the late afternoon. Suddenly there was a cry from the Officer of the Watch.

"Gunboat sighted on starboard side. Distance two miles and closing." The Commander ordered, "Prepare to dive."

The hatch was closed and the vessel flooded her ballast tanks and slowly submerged.

"Like the officer said," commented Wiglington, "nothing odd about diving. Just a little popping of the ears." He shook his head and swallowed.

They were fairly deep now, below the level at which the periscope could be used so they were dependent upon their radar equipment to tell them what was going on. They were receiving radar signals locating the gunboat. There was, of course, no knowing if it was hostile or friendly. Attempts to make radio contact had failed but that was not unusual during a dive, or at the depth at which they were now travelling.

The Commander had taken the decision to submerge to avoid putting Wiglington and Wenks in any danger and to minimise the chance of an incident. They would remain at their present level for some time after they had lost contact with the gunboat, then rise to periscope level and have a good look round before surfacing.

"Marvellous how well hidden we are here below the surface of the water, isn't it?" said Wenks.

"Yes, but the gunboat, or anybody else for that matter, can still locate us with their radar system. They would have a job capturing us, of course," replied Wiglington, "all they could do is blow us up."

"That wouldn't do them much good," replied Wenks, "they want our knowledge, not our dead bodies. How long before we reach Malta?" she enquired.

"About a week," replied Wiglington, "assuming we can sail on the surface most of the time. If we have to proceed submerged we shall be rather slower than that."

As it turned out the gunboat went away and there was no sign of it when they came close to the surface and the periscope was raised. Their journey proceeded without interruption until they were within half a day of Malta.

It was a bright, sunny morning, with hardly a cloud in the sky. Being mid-summer, it was hot. The lookout had reported sighting several ships, which was to be expected in the busy sea lanes around the Mediterranean.

Without warning, over the horizon there appeared a whole flotilla of gunboats, not in formation but ranged on all sides. The lookout counted seven but said there might have been more that were not visible.

"They look like a pack of Sea Wolves," said the lookout. (The Sea Wolves were the Navy arm of the Huntergrunden.)

The Commander ordered a fast dive and within ten minutes the submarine was resting on the bottom of the sea, her engines switched off. In this position she was quite difficult to detect.

Wiglington and Wenks studied the radar screen in the wireless room. They were becoming quite expert at reading the various signals.

"That's a shoal of fish, big ones by the look of it. Dolphin, I expect," said Mallard the short, wiry Radar Operator with an eagle eye, pointing to a series of dots on the viewer, "and there are four of the gunboats," he continued. The other three had apparently left the immediate vicinity and were out of range.

The gunboats seemed to be closing in on the submarine's position.

"If they carry on like that they'll bump each other, won't they?" asked Wiglington.

"They would if they continued at that speed," replied Mallard, "but they'll slow down soon — there, they are losing speed already."

When the four gunboats had assembled immediately above them they stopped. A few minutes later there was a loud *clang* as something hit the side of the submarine.

Wenks jumped. "What was that?" she asked.

"Don't know," replied the sailor, "not a depth charge, obviously. Maybe some kind of sounding apparatus."

All was very still. Even the sailors were quiet. You couldn't hear the gunboat engines. There was an eerie silence. It seemed as if both sides were waiting to see what the other would do.

Then, suddenly, outside the submarine, there was a noise. It was as if someone was speaking with their head in a goldfish bowl. The words were all distorted like a man gargling and talking at the same time. But you could make out what he was saying fairly well.

"This is the Huntergrunden. We know Wiglington and Wenks are down there. We have instructions to present Count Cannaregio's compliments. He would like to see them up here. Now."

"Oh, dear," said Wenks, "and to think we had dinner with that man and I spoke to him most of the evening. I hope I didn't give too much away." She was obviously worried.

"Not at all," said Wiglington reassuringly, "we both acted on Petrov's advice so neither of us is to blame. Besides, how could anyone tell that he was connected with the Huntergrunden?"

The Commander appeared at the door of the Radar Room.

"Well, they didn't take long to find us, did they?" he said cheerily, "all we have to do now is to give them the slip."

"How do you do that?" enquired Wiglington, "I thought they could follow us wherever we moved?"

"Normally that would be true," replied the Commander, "but in our case we have an ingenious new toy developed for us by the Portsmouth Research fellows. It is a very slow moving, unarmed torpedo and it sends out signals just like a submarine. What we do is launch it through one of our torpedo tubes. We remain where we are but send up a small amount of citric acid through the conning tower. Actually," he added, "it's a trade secret

Launching the decoy.

but I think I can tell you. We use Alka-Seltzer tablets. They fizz just before they get to the surface, giving the impression that we are moving. The gunboats then cast about to see which way we are going and they locate the 'dummy' submarine moving away. So they follow that."

"How very clever," said Wiglington, "we did something like that when we wanted to distract the Batpack. In our case we used Castle and Filorat to confuse the enemy. Your system is much more technical, of course."

"When our decoy has drawn them off a fair distance," continued the Commander, "we move stealthily away from here, using our electric motors so as not to make a noise. About two hours later the decoy will have brought the gunboats back to this exact spot. It will then shoot a small flare into the water and release a lot of black ink, which looks like oil. With any luck the gunboats will think we have sunk and go away for a while."

"Ready to launch, Sir," reported Bollard looking round the Radar Room door.

"Launch away," said the Commander, "at slowest speed. This should keep them guessing."

Wiglington and Wenks went to the base of the conning tower to see the other launch — the Alka-Seltzer. It was most impressive.

There must have been over a hundred tablets in the outer sachet that was slipped into the escape hatch.

"That should cure their headache for a while," giggled Wenks, highly taken with the Alka-Seltzer idea.

There was nothing they could do for the next hour except wait. Bollard and Mallard were coming off duty and they invited Wiglington and Wenks to the sailors' mess for a game of draughts and a soft drink.

The sailors had been very kind to them, especially Bollard and Mallard. The former had been detailed off by the Commander to look after them. Bollard and Mallard were great friends so naturally Wiglington and Wenks saw a lot of Mallard, too. Not only that, but Mallard was in charge of the Radar Room, the most exciting place on the submarine as far as Wiglington and Wenks were concerned. They were always popping in to see what the screen was showing. It was better than television.

Wenks noticed that the sailors had smaller quarters than the officers but they were still very comfortable, considering how cramped a submarine is. And Wiglington won his game of draughts against Bollard which pleased him no end.

Having given the gunboats the slip they were ready to complete the last part of the journey.

"We'll go in after dark," said the Commander, "that way we shall not be visible at least until the morning. Of course, it'll mean paying the pilot overtime rates but the Admiralty said no expense was to be spared."

Soon after sunset that evening a half-submerged submarine stole quietly into Valletta harbour, discharged the pilot, flooded her ballast tanks and settled on the bottom to spend the night unseen.

CHAPTER 4

ST PAUL'S ISLAND

For all their special treatment and excellent quarters, Wiglington and Wenks were beginning to feel somewhat like sardines after nine days in the submarine. It wasn't that they were complaining. Not at all. They were very fortunate and knew it. It was just that they missed the country walks and the fresh air and the ability to scamper off anywhere they chose. Suddenly all this was gone. Only for the time being, of course. But they missed it.

On their first morning in port they made their way to the Radar Room to find a very puzzled Mallard.

"Can't fathom this at all," he said to them pointing to the screen. There was a dense mass of dots, quite near the vessel, weaving this way and that.

"It's not dolphin," continued Mallard, "not big enough for them. It might be jellyfish but they don't usually show up on the radar. Minnows I would recognise at once." He scratched his head.

About an hour later, when Wiglington and Wenks were still in the Radar Room and the mysterious blob still hadn't gone away, the Commander appeared. He looked puzzled, too.

"Most extraordinary message from Lenin's tomb. That's our nickname for the Admiralty Plans Division," he explained to them, "says here to look out for a shoal of Lampuki who will guide us to the inner chamber where we will be best protected. What the dickens are Lampuki? Blessed if I know."

"Oh, I know," said Wiglington, "they're a fish. Usually more associated with the table than with pilot duties." Wiglington could be very lucid at times, thought Wenks.

"Oh, I know," said Wiglington, "they're a fish . . . ."

"A fish," mused the Captain, "I see. And how are we supposed to contact these fish, I wonder? My fish-talk is somewhat limited."

"Begging your pardon, Sir," said Mallard, "but maybe there's no need to actually speak to them. Maybe they have been chosen because they respond to flashes from our radar. It's worth a try, anyway, don't you think?"

"Certainly," agreed the Commander.

Mallard sent some signals and watched to see if the shoal responded. Yes, there was a sudden change in the pattern of their weaving. They lined up and moved away from the Repeller. When the ship didn't move, they turned round and came back.

"That's it, Commander," said Mallard, "they want us to follow them."

"I suppose it's safe," said the Commander, "we really ought to satisfy ourselves that they are Lampuki . . . and the ones we are meant to be following. However, I think it is unlikely we shall come to much harm as long as we stay within the harbour."

The necessary signals were sent to notify the Harbour Master of their impending movement and the submarine's electric engines were started. She moved forward very slowly. Once again the radar flashed and the shoal lined up and set off ahead of them. HMS Repeller followed at a snail's pace.

"Steady," muttered Mallard, "we seem to be heading straight for the harbour bastions." It was a tense moment. The Lampuki went ahead. And then, as if out of the blue, the radar screen showed what looked like a tunnel immediately ahead of them.

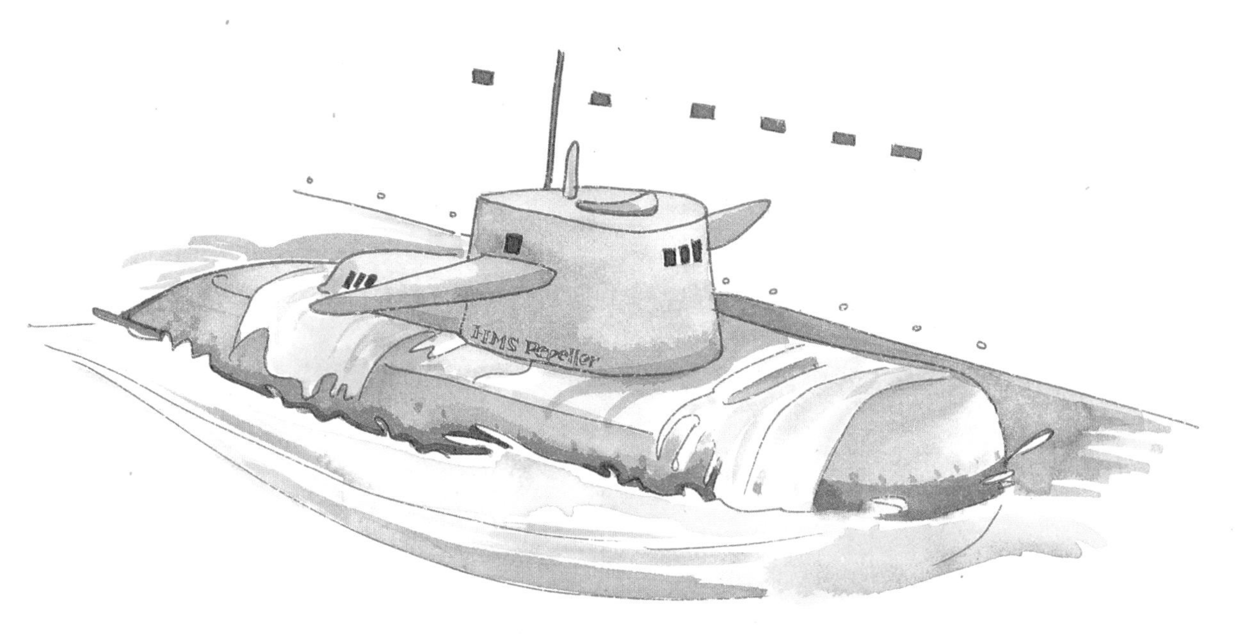

After several minutes inside the mysterious passage it appeared that they were coming out of it into another, more open area.

"Good heavens!" exclaimed the Commander. "A giant underwater drain big enough to hold a submarine. Where do you think that will take us?"

The ship was just inching its way forward now. She was well clear of the sides of this strange, man-made cave but the radar wasn't showing very far ahead and they had to be careful not to damage her by bumping anything.

After several minutes inside the mysterious passage it appeared that they were coming out of it into another, more open area. Soon the Lampuki stopped and the shoal turned round facing the Repeller.

"I think that's it, Sir," said Mallard, "the Lampuki seem to indicate that they have finished their job."

"I wish there was some way we could thank them," replied the Commander, "perhaps another toot on the radar would do it?" Mallard smiled to himself. He had been communicating with Dolphin on the radar for years. The Lampuki were not that different, just smaller. Of course, you never let the officers know you could send signals to fish in case they thought you were mad.

The Commander gave the order to surface slowly and the

submarine heaved herself out of the water. Wiglington and Wenks went on deck with the Commander and the First Officer.

They had been led into an inner harbour, protected all round from outside view. It was quite small. It might have been able to hold three or four submarines but more would have been a tight squeeze.

The harbour was open to the sky but the walls were high above the waterline and you wouldn't have been able to see it unless you were right overhead.

"I've heard about this place," said the Commander, "it was built during the Second World War and was used as a submarine repair base. It even sheltered some submarines when the island was being heavily bombed. It is an ideal place for us to use as our mooring."

"How are we going to get out, though?" asked Wiglington eyeing the high, sheer walls.

"There should be a small doorway in the side," replied the Commander, searching the bastions with his binoculars. "Yes, there it is." He pointed out the escape door. It was alongside the landing jetty, quite hidden against the limestone walls.

"I think we'd better go and explore it," suggested Wiglington.

"I'm afraid you can't do that," replied the Commander, "not until Mr Ruthless and RatGuard have arrived. We have strict instructions that they must escort you at all times when you are not on the submarine. We are obliged always to hand you over to them and receive you back from them. I don't expect them here for another two hours so you'd better come below again and pack a few things. You may be away from the ship for a day or two and you will need your toothbrush and other essentials."

When Mr Ruthless and RatGuard did eventually arrive they came on board to have a chat and see how their charges were. They were horrified to hear of the encounter with the Sea Wolves and made notes of everything. Mr Ruthless said this was the right time to contact Fruba.

"He must be somewhere in the neighbourhood," he said, "we should be able to make contact without too much difficulty."

Mr Ruthless nodded to RatGuard to do the necessary. RatGuard delved into his rucksack and pulled out an extraordinary-looking gadget. It was something they had never seen before — at least, not as an instrument of communication which was clearly what it was meant to be. But it looked, for all the world, like a banana. A biggish banana, mind, with two small dish-like leaves, one at each end. There was even a label on it advertising a well-known banana importer.

Mr Ruthless saw their bemused looks.

"Just something the lab put together for us," he remarked, "we thought as you were upgrading to a submarine we'd better go high-tech too."

Anything less high-tech was difficult to imagine, at least from the outward appearance. You could have carried it in your shopping bag and nobody would have known that it wasn't a banana.

RatGuard pressed the label and immediately the 'banana' sprouted what looked like ears. One had a dial on it, the other, a telephone touch pad.

He moved his dial carefully to locate the nearest satellite and punched out a number on the pad. After two rings a voice answered. It was Fruba.

It took Fruba only a few minutes to arrive at the submarine. He looked tired and slumped into a chair as soon as he had met everyone.

"What with dodging CorporalBat and his lot and trying to locate the Huntergrunden, I'm all in," he complained.

"Had any luck?" asked Mr Ruthless, anxious to get down to business.

"Yes," replied Fruba, "Sea Wolf Pack is headed towards Malta. Apparently they were under the impression that you had sunk. They are reported to have said that they saw the debris coming to the surface."

"Alka-Seltzer," muttered Wiglington to Wenks.

"Later, they found out that you were safe and sound and now they are on their way."

"When do you expect them to make landfall?" asked Mr Ruthless.

"'Bout four hours," replied Fruba, "so there is still time to do some exploring before they arrive."

"However," he continued, "CorporalBat is already here, ahead of them. He has set up his command in the Castille Tower which gives him an excellent view of Valletta. It will be difficult to move about unseen. We may need to resort to disguise. By the way," he added, "the Ratbag has arrived as well. My chaps signalled that they had found a very satisfactory and discreet landing place at Floriana, not too far from here. We should only use the vehicle when we really need it, though. Once its cover is blown it will be difficult to hide it."

"Where do you want to begin looking?" asked RatGuard.

"Sir Ordy told us that the last maps we found suggested that the best clues we are likely to get in Malta will come from Mdina Cathedral. We should go there and call upon the Archbishop. He will surely know the history of Carto Wiglington's map of Malta."

"Here's what I suggest, then," said Fruba, "I shall go to the Castille Tower and conduct a one-bat bombing raid. It will distract CorporalBat who doesn't yet know that I am here. While CorporalBat's lot are fending me off, you slink out and make your way to Mdina."

It seemed a good idea so the plan was put into action.

Archbishop Candlesticks was a very jolly man, plump and smiling. He enjoyed an occasional chocolate. Kind and gentle, he nevertheless had a strong will which he exercised in the interests of the Maltese who loved and respected him greatly. His influence was felt well beyond Mdina, beyond even Malta, and it was said that the Vatican often consulted him on matters concerning the church.

He invited Wiglington and Wenks to have lunch with him on the terrace of his house in the cathedral precinct. It was a hot, sunny day and they sat under the vines and the wisteria enjoying cold spring lamb and raspberry salad, an unusual but mouth-watering combination. The raspberries had been dressed in a vinaigrette sauce so light that they retained their special taste while having just a hint of cider and olive oil.

The Archbishop knew the history not only of Carto Wiglington's map but also of Malta. And he loved telling people about the country with its rich background. It had been occupied by many races — the Phoenicians, the Carthaginians, the Romans, and most recently by the British who had remained until independence in 1974.

The repeated infusion of new ideas and cultures had added to the artistic and creative spirit of the Maltese people who had managed to assimilate them while at the same time remain very much their own race.

"Bit like Bentley," observed Wiglington, "they come and go often enough there but it doesn't affect us much."

"I think the cultural influences were a little more profound here," admonished Wenks who thought Wiglington was taking it all a trifle frivolously.

Archbishop Candlesticks was amused by the couple. Where else in the world would you find yourself discussing the finer points of Malta's cartographic history with two English Water Rats?

Archbishop Candlesticks was amused by the couple.

After taking them through the various stages of Malta's evolution the Archbishop addressed himself to the problem they were most anxious to solve.

"I have never seen the Carto Wiglington map of Malta," he said in a definitive sort of way, "but I do know that there is one. In fact," he continued, "I believe there may be more than one." He paused. Wiglington and Wenks leant forward in their chairs.

"Remember," he went on, "that there are three islands here — Malta, Gozo and Comino. Malta is the biggest by a long way, of course, but the other islands also have an interesting history. It seems improbable that he would have forgotten them, doesn't it?"

Wiglington and Wenks nodded. All that they had learned about Carto Wiglington led them to believe that he was not a forgetful fellow.

The Archbishop went on, "The map or maps have not appeared in the cathedral archives or I should have heard about it. But that isn't to say that there aren't clues as to their whereabouts. When you have had enough lunch we shall investigate."

They enjoyed a helping of goat's milk cheese with its strong, pungent smell and flavour. Then the Archbishop introduced them to what Wiglington and Wenks thought must have been the most delectable chocolate cake in the world. They finished off with a cup of coffee — the best cappuccino that Wenks could remember, even including Italy. 'Aha,' they thought to themselves, 'now for the cathedral and the clues.'

Alas it was not to be just yet. First there was the essential siesta. Wiglington and Wenks admitted that, with the sun so hot in the middle of the day and the early afternoon, work was not at the top of the agenda and forty winks in the shade put things right for a burst of feverish activity lasting as long as an hour in between the afternoon sleep and the evening meal.

The Archbishop put his feet up on a cane chair, pulled his skullcap forward over his eyes and dozed as he had done at this time of day for the last twenty years. Wiglington and Wenks curled up and followed his example. All was still and peaceful and the thoughts of the Huntergrunden slipped easily away from their minds.

"Wake up, Wiglington," said Wenks, coming to with a start. Wiglington sat up and rubbed his eyes. The Archbishop had gone.

"We'd better go and look for him," he said, jumping down from the chair.

They found Archbishop Candlesticks in the cathedral museum. He had already started the hunt for clues to the whereabouts of the next map. The museum was housed in a building that appeared to have been a private house in the not too distant past. They climbed the elegant staircase with its wrought-iron banister to the first floor. A museum library occupied the first room and there, in the middle of it, stood Archbishop Candlesticks busily searching through the shelves. Wiglington and Wenks lent a hand.

"What exactly are we looking for?" asked Wiglington.

"Any book on 13th Century Maps or Old Maps or Ancient Maps," replied the Archbishop, "these books are not arranged in any special order so we will just have to look all the way through."

They found several books that seemed to be relevant, but they all turned out to have nothing about Carto Wiglington in them. Then the Archbishop suggested that they look through the boxes of old prints.

"They're mostly pictures," he said, "but there are some maps among them, I think."

They didn't find a Carto Wiglington map there either but they did see a symbol that looked rather as though it might have been Carto's signature. It was on a map of the tiny island known as St Paul's, believed to be the place where the saint was shipwrecked. You couldn't quite make out the squiggles because they were right where anyone holding the map would place his thumb. But squiggles there were and it was the only lead they had.

Getting to St Paul's Island the next day meant a short boat ride. The sea was choppy and the landing stage, primitive. Every time the boatman brought his craft near, the swell made it impossible to reach the little jetty. In the end Wiglington and Wenks changed into their bathing costumes and swam ashore. Fruba flew with them, quite the hero for having successfully distracted CorporalBat and his gang yesterday, while RatGuard stayed on the boat with Mr Ruthless.

Getting to St Paul's Island the next day meant a short boat ride.

Wiglington and Wenks went to the spot where the squiggles had been marked on the map. It was the most rugged part of the island, all rocks and tiny caves. Birds nested precariously on the cliffs.

Wiglington and Wenks went into the first cave, and then the second. They had barely entered the third and were looking at some interesting signs on the walls when they heard a cry from Fruba.

They rushed outside just in time to see him being carried off by CorporalBat and several of his cronies. He was squawking and looking back at them, calling for help. But there was nothing they could do.

As they stood there watching, a small gunboat appeared on the horizon. It was heading straight for St Paul's Island.

CHAPTER 5

HIEROGLYPHICS

"We have very little time," observed Wiglington, as usual making the obvious sound like news, "we must find out what those markings are on the cave wall and get out of here fast."

They had just turned to go back into the cave when Wenks let out a small scream.

"Look," she said pointing to the edge of the cliff, "look at that baby bird. He's much too young to fly and he's going to fall. See, his mother is trying to rescue him but she can't reach him."

Wiglington knew what had to be done. He leapt across the rocks as fast as his paws would carry him, balancing carefully each time he landed.

He got to where the baby Merril was, and caught it as it was tipping over the edge. The infant bird shrieked and shut its eyes. Wiglington climbed carefully up the side of the cliff and gave the squawking brat back to its mother.

She was overjoyed.

"Oh, I can't thank you enough," she said, "you were so brave. Bless you, Sir." Wiglington was quite embarrassed.

"Oh, it was nothing really," he replied, "and now, if you will forgive me I am in rather a hurry." He was about to leave when the Merril spoke again.

"Is there anything I can do to thank you? *Anything* at all?" she asked.

"As a matter of fact," replied Wiglington, "now that you mention it, there is. If you could get your friends and neighbours here to make a concerted attack on that boat approaching the island it might keep them at bay long enough for us to complete our work and make our escape."

"Delighted," replied the Merril, "and so will all the others be. That's a Sea Wolf boat and we don't want them messing around here. They steal our eggs and kill our young and leave empty soft drink cans on the beach when they depart. We'll go and harass them immediately. How long will you want?"

"Only about fifteen minutes, I think," replied Wiglington, "and thank you very much."

"On the contrary," said the Merril, "thank *you*."

Wiglington thought these thanks might go on for a long time so he returned to the third cave and scampered inside with Wenks, to look again at the signs.

He got to where the baby Merril was, and caught it as it was tipping over the edge.

They were in a strange language which neither of them could understand so they hastily made as good a copy of them as they could, given the shortage of time. Here is what they jotted down.

Here is what they jotted down.

They had no idea who might be able to interpret this. Perhaps kind Archbishop Candlesticks would know what it meant.

For now, their priority was escape and they bundled themselves back through the mouth of the cave, dived into the water and swam for all they were worth back to the boat.

In spite of all the efforts of the flock of Merrils, the Sea Wolf boat had got perilously close by now. It was a powerful machine, noisy and menacing. The little boat that Wiglington and Wenks had taken to the island had no chance in a race between the two. They had barely started their journey back to Valletta when the Sea Wolf spotted them. She turned her bow, opened her throttles and raced towards them as if intent on a head-on collision.

Wiglington and Wenks were horrified. RatGuard was talking feverishly into his bananaphone, but then he had been doing that ever since they had reached the island and it didn't seem to have produced any results so far. Things looked bad. Even Wenks had to admit that.

And then an amazing thing happened.

The sea started to froth, quite close to their boat. Great white plumes of bubbles rose into the air and, suddenly, what looked like a giant, black whale heaved its way ponderously to the surface.

HMS Repeller had made it just in time.

The Sea Wolf slowed and reversed her motors to bring her to an abrupt halt. For a moment she looked lost. Then she turned tail and fled, pursued by the submarine now bent on capture.

But an old submarine is not a fast ship and once the Sea Wolf had turned round her power soon saw her well clear and heading once again for the horizon.

Wiglington and Wenks were speechless. Whoever that chap Major Consideration was, he had certainly seen to it that they were well protected. They breathed a sigh of relief.

A loud-hailer called from the submarine. "If you can swim to us we'll take you on board." Wiglington and Wenks needed no second invitation. Without asking RatGuard's opinion they dived in and swam for the Repeller. A rope ladder was slung alongside and in no time at all they were descending through the conning tower into the welcome retreat of familiar, and safe, surroundings. It might be like a sardine can but it was a mighty dependable one.

Back on board the Commander summoned them to his cabin. He asked them if they were all right and gave them cocoa and biscuits to ward off the shock of their most recent adventure.

"I think we are going to have to stay closer to you," he said when they had settled down. "We don't want another episode like that, do we?"

Wiglington and Wenks agreed. But they were most anxious about the markings they had seen on the cave.

"We've got to get these interpreted quickly," said Wiglington, "or the Sea Wolf pack will be there first. After all, they know we were on the island and it is so small that it wouldn't take them too long to find the same cave."

The Commander looked at their copy of the markings. He scratched his head.

"Looks more like a drawing of a cat than anything else to me," he said, "I think there's only one person who might be able to deal with that. He's a very clever man and he happens to be visiting here at present. Actually, this is his original home but he seems to live all over the world nowadays. One of his schools is in Venice."

Wiglington and Wenks looked at each other.

"You're not talking about the Genius, are you?" they asked together.

"Why, do you know him?" enquired the Commander.

"Oh, yes," replied Wiglington, "we are on what you might call 'ink' terms."

The Commander looked puzzled. They explained how Wenks had had to pour ink onto the Genius's trousers to distract him when they were being overheard by the Batpack on Litteral Thinking Island. The Commander laughed.

"Poor Genius," he said, "I expect he remembers you pretty well, then."

After more discussion they agreed that a visit to the Genius was next on the cards. Messages were sent in code back to the harbour to make the necessary arrangements and the Repeller set out on the return journey to her berth.

"We mustn't forget Fruba," said Wenks suddenly. The excitement of the past hour had pushed the plight of the Fruit Bat out of their minds. "How do you think we should set about getting a search party going, Wiglington?" she asked.

"Haven't a clue," replied Wiglington, "perhaps a word with Bollard and Mallard will not be out of place." They were sitting in their cabin after changing into dry clothes. Wiglington took the ship's phone off the hook and blew into it.

"Why did you do that?" enquired Wenks, amused.

"I thought you always had to blow into ship's phones. I distinctly remember seeing that happen in a film about the First World War." He seemed a bit put out.

"Not today, silly," replied Wenks, laughing gently at him,

"that was years ago. Now they have all modern electronics. Just press the button."

Bollard was summoned and, on his arrival, briefed about Fruba.

"We'll get a couple of observers up to the Castille Tower," he promised, "and see if we can find out where they've taken him. In the meantime, no going ashore without the Commander's permission and a full escort. We don't want you exposed to danger again and we can't always get the sub out at short notice. Your last escapade gave us quite a turn, you know."

By the time the Repeller was back at her berth the reconnaissance team had returned. They had disturbing news. Fruba had been taken to the Castille Tower and bound and gagged. He was locked in the safe room in the tower. Only a miracle could set him free.

"We must try," insisted Wenks, "after all, he is supposed to be on our side and all our doubts about him have been founded on the flimsiest of speculation. When it comes right down to it he has done everything we could have expected of him."

"Apart from having terribly bad luck with monotonous regularity," observed Wiglington sarcastically. Wenks frowned at him. This was not like Wiglington. Usually he gave everyone the benefit of the doubt but he seemed to have it in for Fruba. She felt sorry for the chap.

"But I suppose you're right," Wiglington went on, "only question is how to get him freed. Do you think we might enlist the services of the crew of HMS Repeller?" he addressed the question to Bollard.

"I'll ask the Commander," replied Bollard.

The Commander was doubtful.

"We were detailed to look after Wiglington and Wenks, not the Fruit Bats. If we take on more where will it end? We could be responsible for half the wildlife in the world."

Wenks looked sad and went over to the Commander. Her big, brown eyes filled with tears as she looked up at him.

"If it was you who was locked up and bound and gagged,

Wenks looked sad and went over to the Commander.

we'd come after you. We wouldn't abandon you to . . . ," her voice trailed away. It was as if she was unable to finish the sentence.

'Oh, my ears and whiskers,' thought Wiglington, 'Wenks! Innocent, simple Wenks has got the Commander of a submarine wrapped round her little finger. Let's see if he can talk his way out of this one.'

Naturally the Commander, being a gentleman, gave in and a party set out from the submarine base as soon as darkness fell. The Commander decided to come with them, leaving Mr Bellows to mind the ship. Bollard and Mallard were obvious candidates for the venture. Four other sailors were pressed into service by the Master at Arms and Mr Ruthless and RatGuard were well to the fore. With Wiglington and Wenks that made eleven altogether.

They must have made the pirates of old look like a Sunday School outing by comparison.

They were armed with anti-batdropping missiles and they carried long ropes and hooks with which to scale the tower. They took along an emergency kit to attend to Fruba's wounds and those of any casualties they might sustain. The Commander had hired a jeep to transport them and Wiglington and Wenks stood on the top of the driver's seat backrest, clinging to the bar that supported the roof of the vehicle.

"Forward," cried the Commander and Bollard, who was driving, let in the clutch with such ferocity that it was all that our friends could do to hang on.

The jeep climbed the steep bastions of Valletta and wound its way up to the tower. There was a lot of feverish activity there as the Prime Minister was just leaving his office which was nearby. They waited politely for him to go. Then the jeep slipped round to the back of the tower and the action began.

CHAPTER 6

FRUBA AND THE CHAIR

Fruba was dazed. The events of the past few hours had been so fast and frightening that he could hardly recall them.

There had been the mission to St Paul's Island. Obviously Wiglington and Wenks had found something of interest there. He was just going to explore it when *wham*! CorporalBat and his cronies appeared on the scene. He hadn't stood a chance.

The capture had been swift. He was on his way back to the Castille Tower before you could say Gozo. CorporalBat had not been considerate. He had treated Fruba quite roughly. He demanded to know why Fruba had teamed up with Wiglington and Wenks. He insisted on being told the whereabouts of the maps, even though Fruba genuinely did not know. He even threatened Fruba with what he described as 'dire consequences' if he didn't change sides immediately and co-operate with CorporalBat.

Fruba had remained sullenly silent up to this point. Suddenly he got angry.

"You will regret this insubordination, CorporalBat," he warned, "you may have the upper hand now but wait, the tables will be turned and you will be given the 'Ultimate Penalty'."

That made CorporalBat stop and think.

The 'Ultimate Penalty' for a Fruit Bat is to have to spend the rest of his life in an upright position and never again to be able to hang upside down. It is the worst punishment that can be inflicted. Apart from extreme discomfort, it causes endless headaches and very sore feet.

But CorporalBat was in so much trouble anyway. 'May as well be unhung for a sheep as for a lamb' — he recited the old Fruit Bat saying to himself.

"You won't survive this ordeal, Fruba," he said menacingly. He ordered his men to bind and gag Fruba and left him to consider his fate.

CorporalBat was taking a nap when the attack began. The first he knew of it was a shout which woke him with a start. One of his men on sentry duty had spotted the hook of a grappling iron. It was caught on the window ledge in the room next to where Fruba was lying. From the way it kept getting tense and then loose it seemed to be in use. He peered over the side.

Sure enough, a swarthy character, dressed all in black, was climbing the rope. He wore a helmet as though prepared for battle.

"Boarders ahoy!" CorporalBat shouted, "Prepare to repel boarders!"

His team went into action immediately. Batdroppings showered on the invaders. They needed their helmets for sure.

Fruba heard the commotion. He had been working on the ropes that bound him and had succeeded in loosening them somewhat. Now he redoubled his efforts and managed to break the manacle, freeing his wings. It was but a few seconds work to remove the gag and he was mobile again. He thought carefully. The time at which he could be most useful to his rescuers would be when they were almost at the top of the tower and about to leap across, into the room. If he could put CorporalBat's fellows out of action at that point he would indeed have helped.

There was a chair in the corner of the room. He picked it up and hurled it with all his might against the wall. Two of the legs came away from the seat. They made excellent truncheons. Now for CorporalBat.

Fruba chose his moment precisely. Then he pounced.

Flinging open the door of the adjacent room he threw himself furiously on the first figure he saw, pounding for all he was worth. It positively rained blows.

Poor Bollard. He had expected ferocity from the Fruit Bats. He was, after all, equipped to put up with a fair amount of it. But never in his wildest dreams did he expect such force. He quite lost his breath.

Meanwhile Wiglington appeared over the edge of the tower parapet. He saw immediately what was happening.

"Stop, Fruba," he called, "you are fighting the wrong person." Fruba just managed to restrain the next blow aimed at Bollard's not insubstantial neck.

"Oh, my goodness! What have I done?" cried Fruba. "Here, let me help you. Come, sit down." He fetched the seat of the chair he had so recently smashed. There were still two legs on it.

Bollard could hardly see. He had covered his face with his hands to fend off any more blows that might come his way. Fruba guided him to the chair. Bollard sat down.

The chair had not been of strong construction in the first place. Fruba's abusive treatment had knocked out of it whatever remaining resilience it might have had. Bollard was no lightweight.

"Stop, Fruba," he called, "you are fighting the wrong person."

The chair yielded with a sort of groan, followed by a sharp crack. Bollard hit the floor with a bang. One of the remaining chair legs ended up sticking in his left ear. He was not a happy sailor.

The members of CorporalBat's team were overcome more by hysterics at the antics of Fruba than by the assault made on them by the sailors. They fell about laughing. Even CorporatBat, not known for his sense of humour, had to smile.

But the battle was not yet done. As soon as everyone had recovered from the fracas, they set to again. This time Fruba managed to see that he was on the right side and, with the aid of a not-too-enchanted Bollard, they got him to the rope and persuaded him to slide down it. By the time he reached the bottom there was a slight smell of burning flesh where the rope had cut into his claws. He looked a wreck.

The others made their escape without further ado and the party retreated, not without the odd batdropping attack, to the submarine and relative sanity.

A doctor examined Fruba as soon as they got on board. His prognosis was not encouraging.

"Total nervous breakdown, mouth full of ulcers, burnt claws, poor general condition," he diagnosed, continuing, "treatment, complete rest, no activity, cod liver oil taken internally and externally three times a day." Fruba felt this was not going to be much fun but he was in such rotten shape that he didn't have the strength to protest.

So for the next few days Fruba was confined to his hammock which, of course, hung upside down. They all went to visit him from time to time and brought him the latest news on what was happening. Even Bollard called on him but he insisted that Wiglington went into Fruba's cabin first. He didn't want another beating.

Mr Ruthless summoned a conference.

"They're more organised than I gave them credit for," he said, referring to the Huntergrunden, "Count Cannaregio is here on the island. They already have a map. I don't know where it is but

I do know that it's not at the Castille Tower. They're too smart for that."

Mr Ruthless mopped his brow. It was all getting a bit much, he thought.

"It seems that we are going to have a difficult task locating our map. We don't even know how many there are but the best clue I have so far is that one of them may well be in the Hypogeum in Paola."

"Surely our coded message from St Paul's Island will help us?" interjected Wiglington.

"Steady, steady," replied Mr Ruthless, "one thing at a time. We shan't get the hieroglyphics interpreted until we see the Genius. He's here at present and I have arranged a meeting with him later on today. We shall have to be careful getting there because the Huntergrunden are aware of your support and they are strengthening their forces to combat the Navy."

The Commander intervened.

"If I may say so," he said, "I think you need a dose of Navy organisation about all this. Of course," he continued, "it's none of my business but it seems to me that you have several things to do and limited time and resources with which to do them. Just the same as commanding a submarine, really."

They all nodded, encouraging him to go on.

"Which is the more important?" he asked, "getting to the map or maps that the Huntergrunden do not have or getting to the one they do have? Obviously," he went on without a pause, "getting to the maps they don't have. The map in the possession of the Huntergrunden isn't likely to go away. Even if they move it, it will still be under their control. But they will be looking for the maps they don't have and it is important for you to find these first. So, my conclusion is that you should get to see the Genius right away and give no hostages to fortune until you have done so."

Mr Ruthless applauded the Commander's clear analysis and asked how soon they could be ready to go to meet the Genius.

Later that day HMS Repeller set off underwater, using only her batteries to power the propellers. She slipped through what they had all come to call 'the drain' and manoeuvred her way out of the harbour, her periscope just above waterline.

After further discussion with the Genius it had been decided that his home was too obvious a place to meet. The Hunter-grunden would surely be staking it out. A rendezvous at the southern tip of the island was chosen.

Marsaxlokk is Malta's premier fishing village. It has a busy, bustling Sunday market and some excellent restaurants whose speciality is, of course, seafood. The rendezvous had been set for Ir Rizzu, a popular local restaurant.

The submarine got them as close to the shore as she could, out of view of the main quay with its bustle and activity. The final approach would be made by rubber dingy rowed by Bollard and Mallard.

Wiglington and Wenks peered anxiously over the bow of the little boat. Mr Ruthless and RatGuard watched through their bin-oculars, scanning the horizon to see if there was anything to cause alarm. All seemed set fair.

CHAPTER 7

THE GENIUS INTERPRETS

The Genius was waiting for them. He smiled when he saw them come through the door of the restaurant. Their sailor suits and hats made them look quite a lot bigger than when he had seen them on Litteral Thinking Island. They looked somehow more worldly, more experienced.

The first thing Wenks noticed was that the Genius was wearing dark trousers. He obviously hadn't forgotten the episode of the spilled ink. But he didn't mention it, of course. Just steered well clear of any liquid that was sitting around.

After they had all said hello, the Genius told them of the consequences of the false trail they had laid when leaving Venice. In order to put the Batpack off the scent the CORGIS had leaked the misinformation that the Carto Wiglington map was on Litteral Thinking Island. The Batpack had planned an attack and had carried it out the very day that Wiglington and Wenks had departed for Rome.

As soon as the doors of the lecture hall had been opened the Fruit Bats had poured in on all sides. A mighty battle had ensued because there was a particularly tough bunch of students studying there at the time.

"There was total chaos," recalled the Genius, smiling, "but the students won in the end and the Batpack beat a hasty retreat. Actually," he continued, "they were a difficult group of pupils to start with but after the Batpack raid they settled down and became most attentive. It just goes to show the value of a common enemy."

Wiglington and Wenks felt most embarrassed to have been the cause of so much trouble but the Genius put them at their ease. He seemed to have rather enjoyed the whole thing.

When they had all got the food they wanted, Wiglington showed the Genius his sketch of the wall writings in the cave on St Paul's Island. The Genius studied them for a moment.

"Did you see any other wall markings in the cave?" he enquired.

"No," replied Wiglington, "but we were very short of time. The Huntergrunden were on our tail and we had but a few moments to make a copy."

"Not only that," chipped in Wenks, "but most of the time we did have, Wiglington was busy rescuing a baby Merril which was about to fall to its death."

"I only ask," continued the Genius, "because obviously Carto Wiglington thought that the cave was a good place to leave messages. It seems likely that the map was moved a number of times, the latest location being recorded in the cave. If my idea is correct there may be messages there about Carto's other maps in Malta."

He turned his attention to Wiglington's reproduction of the cave drawings.

"Definitely looks like a cat, almost has a Cheshire cat grin, doesn't it?" he mused. "But what is this strange looking thing on the side?"

They all peered over his shoulder.

"A sort of ladder with one of the long bits missing," said Wiglington, trying to be helpful.

"Looks more like a giant comb to me," replied Wenks. The Genius sat up.

"Of course," he exclaimed, "once you say that you've solved the mystery. 'Cat and comb' can only mean one thing 'Catacomb'. I'll bet the map was hidden in the catacombs at Rabat in St Paul's or St Agatha's, hence the connection. We shall go there after lunch and see if we can trace it."

The Genius became very excited and hurried them through the rest of their meal so that they could be on the trail quickly. He had a rickety old car which coped well with the potholes of the Malta roads. He offered to drive Wiglington and Wenks, Mr Ruthless and RatGuard over to Rabat. Bollard and Mallard would take the dinghy back to the submarine and await a call from RatGuard about the movements planned for after the visit to the catacombs.

Bollard and Mallard were not happy with the arrangement. The Commander had given them strict instructions to keep a close watch on Wiglington and Wenks and they obviously couldn't do that if they were rowing out to sea on their own. On the other hand they couldn't fit into the car either. There was nothing for it but to find a way of carrying out their instructions without upsetting the Genius.

They watched as the car sped away, the Genius at the wheel determined to lose no time in getting to Rabat. They glanced around. They were in luck. A taxi approached, crawling along slowly as if seeking a fare. They waved. The taxi stopped. Bollard opened the door and was just climbing in when he saw that it was already occupied.

"That's all right, sailor," said the occupant, "jump aboard. I'm in no hurry and I can easily give you and your friend a lift."

They watched as the car sped away, the Genius at the wheel determined to lose no time in getting to Rabat.

"Very kind of you, Sir," replied Bollard as he and Mallard scrambled into the car. It was a tight squeeze. Neither of the sailors was small. The Italian, for that is what he seemed to be, was also a big fellow. He grinned at them as the vehicle sped away. Mallard thought it strange that the driver moved off without being told where they were going. Perhaps Bollard had said something as he boarded.

"Rabat, please," requested Bollard, further confusing his colleague. The driver said nothing.

"Are you on holiday?" enquired the Italian.

"No, actually," replied Mallard, "we're working. Very special duty." Bollard looked daggers at him and Mallard shut up.

"Where are you from?" Bollard asked the Italian, changing the subject.

"Oh I come from Venice," he replied, "but I'm often in Malta these days. I have some work here, you see." He grinned again.

"I am going to Rabat myself," said the Italian, "what would you be going there for?"

"To see some friends," replied Bollard hastily. He didn't want Mallard giving away anything about their mission.

"Friends in search of something, are they?" leered the Italian. "Friends looking for a map, by any chance?" His face became positively contorted.

Bollard and Mallard remained silent. This was turning nasty.

"I am Count Cannaregio," said the Italian suddenly, "and I know who you are. You are the sailors sent to look after Wiglington and Wenks. How much do you get paid?"

Bollard and Mallard didn't answer.

"I can offer you a great deal more, whatever it is," the Count continued, "in fact, I can make you rich. Very rich." He reached into the inside pocket of his coat and pulled out a handful of bank notes. He crinkled them temptingly.

"All you have to do," he went on, "is to let me know when they locate the map. I'll do the rest. You'll collect the loot." He crinkled again.

Now Bollard and Mallard had been chosen for the job because they were loyal sailors. They could not be bought. But as they listened to the Count they both thought what an opportunity this was for them to find out what the enemy was doing. By merely agreeing to what the Count was suggesting they could help Wiglington and Wenks with vital information, especially about where the Huntergrunden's own Carto Wiglington map was.

"I'd consider it," said Bollard, "if the price is right."

"I shall see to it that a considerable sum of money is placed in an agreed safe haven for you if you tell me when the Rats have found their next map. I will give you the secret number to reach me direct."

Mallard realised what Bollard was doing and nodded his approval.

Count Cannaregio seemed satisfied with their intentions and set them down in Rabat. He had given them the contact number. As far as he was concerned they were on his team now.

CHAPTER 8

IN THE CATACOMBS

You need a good guide in the underground passages in Rabat. They are narrow, low and exceedingly damp. They show the burial places of many good souls whose purpose, one feels sure, is resting in peace and not being a tourist attraction.

"Eerie, isn't it?" remarked Wenks as they stumbled past the remains of many mortals long since dead.

"Not particularly," contradicted Wiglington, "the mortal remains don't reflect the spirit which I am sure moved on to another plane. We all have to face mortality sometime." Wiglington could be quite morbid, Wenks thought.

"What are we looking for?" she asked with determination.

"A map," replied Wiglington, unusually rudely.

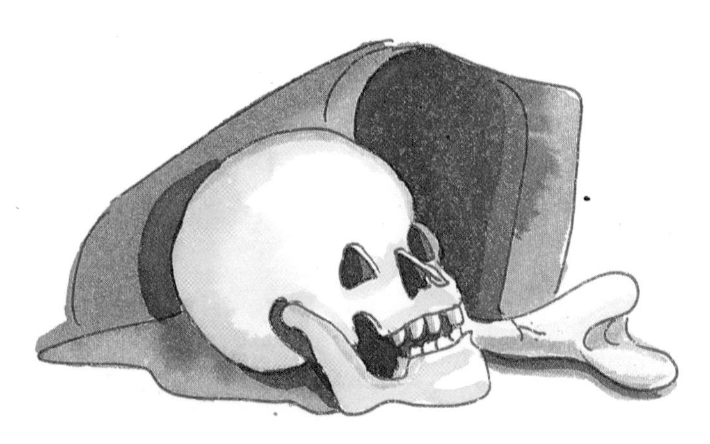

"Eerie, isn't it?" remarked Wenks as they stumbled past the remains of many mortals long since dead.

"Yes, Wiglington," said Wenks, "I know that. But failing the immediate and miraculous appearance of one, what else should we be seeking?"

"Any sign of ancient writing," replied Wiglington, repentant of his bad manners, adding, "any hieroglyphics which could possibly be a clue."

As they got further into the catacombs the air became more musty and the damp, more penetrating. Small bats flew in and out of the tunnels letting out their piercing shrieks which Wiglington and Wenks could hear but which the human visitors couldn't.

The Genius was obviously well known in this subterranean world. Guides greeted him as they passed by. Every now and then a tourist would break away from his group and come and have a word with him.

The journey was slow. Almost every catacomb had some writing on its walls and the Genius had to translate and ponder on whether it was significant. Eventually he called them over.

"Look," he said, "here is a sign very similar to the one you found on St Paul's Island.

"Look," he said, "here is a sign very similar to the one you found on St Paul's Island. There is a distinct outline of a cat but no comb. In this case the cat seems to be sitting on the top of some pedestal. What do you suppose that means?" He looked at Wenks. She had cottoned onto the main point on the previous occasion and she seemed to have a 'crossword' mind.

Wenks thought hard.

"What's another word for pedestal?" she asked, "something like victory or triumph?"

The Genius began to recite all the words he could think of that fitted. "Reward, medal, trophy, achievement . . . ," he stopped. "Just a minute," he said, "cat and trophy. Catastrophe. That must be it, surely. Where do we find the record of a catastrophe down here?"

"I saw a sign some way back there saying that it was the burial site of the victims of the Bugibba Catastrophe," replied Wiglington, "could that be it, do you think?"

They hurried back to the place Wiglington had seen. There were lots of skeletons there, grinning up from their resting places. At the back of each one was a small cubicle, sometimes locked, often open, containing some memento presumably of the person whose remains lay below. One place was empty as if waiting for an occupant. The cubicle door, however, was ajar and a wooden parchment container was just visible in the dim light.

The Genius reached over and took it out. He opened the case and removed the contents. It was a Carto Wiglington map. They all gave a little cheer.

The map was of Valletta. It showed the city in a way which brought to life the early development of the Grand Harbour and the narrow busy streets.

The Genius gave the map to Wiglington and Wenks and was about to pass them the scroll-holder when he noticed a small piece of writing on one end. Carved into the hard wood of the cylindrical box was the word Tarxien. Now the Tarxien Neolithic Temples are a very important ancient site in Malta. The writing on the scroll-case must mean either that the map had been housed there at some stage or that another map was there.

They took the map and case to the curator of the catacombs and explained their mission. He knew the Genius and so was confident about the authenticity of their claim. Releasing the map would, he feared, take a little while since he had to apply to the Minister of Antiquities and Museums whose department was not known for instant decisions. However, he promised that the matter would be addressed with all possible urgency.

Wiglington and Wenks thanked the curator and the Genius and prepared to move off towards the car for a return to HMS Repeller.

Imagine their surprise when they surfaced from the catacombs to find Bollard and Mallard waiting for them. The two sailors looked distressed.

"We thought we'd lost you," said Bollard, stepping forward to make sure they were all right.

Reassured, they decided that Wiglington and Wenks should return to the submarine with them while the Genius should take RatGuard and Mr Ruthless back separately.

Bollard hailed a taxi, failing to notice that it was the very same taxi that had brought them and Count Cannaregio to Rabat.

On the journey, they told Wiglington and Wenks of their meeting with the Count and what they had agreed to do in order to infiltrate the Huntergrunden.

The driver of the taxi couldn't help overhearing them. He turned his head, saying, "Count Cannaregio is an evil man. He destroyed my brother by getting him involved in smuggling and left him to rot in jail. His headquarters in Malta is quite near here. I'd like to help. What can I do? Shall I take you there?"

"Yes," replied Wiglington suddenly, realising what an opportunity he had at hand, "and we'll see if we can locate the map they own."

The taxi swerved off the main highway onto a side road leading to Wardija. Before they realised what was happening it came to rest near a large, castle-like house. The name on the gate said 'Il Palazzo dei Lupi' which means 'The Palace of the Wolves'.

They all got out and the taxi driver showed them a small alcove behind a perfumed oleandar bush where they could hide

The hall was full.

and eavesdrop without being seen. They had a good view of what was going on.

Beyond the little entrance lobby was a vast hall with the biggest fireplace Wiglington and Wenks had ever seen. Over it hung an enormous stag's head.

The hall was full. At a raised table sat Count Cannaregio. Alongside him was another man and two wolves. The wolves sat on the floor with their heads resting on the green baize with which the table was covered.

Facing them was a crowd made up of people, mostly men, and wolves. They could see the odd large dog, too. The Count was speaking.

". . . already had a lot of inefficiency in the Malta Branch," he said angrily, "I won't tolerate any more. The Rats have slipped through our fingers enough times. All due to sloppy planning and poor communication. Got to pull our socks up and get organised."

The audience shuffled uncomfortably. They looked a swarthy lot. There were a few big Alaskan Wolves and a contingent that clearly came from Siberia. There were mercenary soldiers, drop-outs, probably, from armies around the world.

A tall, blond-haired man stood up and spoke with a Scandinavian accent.

"Trouble is that HQ doesn't pass on information," he complained. "We could easily handle the Rats and the whole Royal Navy if our intelligence was better. What are you going to do to improve it?"

Count Cannaregio whispered something to two of his assistants who moved away.

"We think our intelligence is fine," he replied, "it's the people who receive it who are the problem. They have no common sense." Clearly the Count was not best pleased.

A minute later the two assistants appeared by the side of the tall blond-haired man and marched him stiffly away. A scream of terror echoed through the building, demonstrating his fate in no uncertain terms.

Bollard and Mallard beckoned to Wiglington and Wenks to

follow them and they slipped away as fast as they could, before they were discovered.

They returned to the submarine a little shaken but none the worse for their adventure.

Everyone agreed that Bollard and Mallard should use their special position as the Count's official spies to lay a false trail and, more importantly, to find out where the Huntergrunden's map was kept.

As soon as they contacted the Count he wanted to see them, thinking that they had some valuable information for him. Bollard and Mallard made their way to the Palazzo.

On arrival they discovered that the agenda had moved on. From the discussions taking place it became clear that the thrust of the Huntergrunden's work was smuggling and piracy. It sounded like big business.

The gunboats which had been so troublesome to HMS Repeller were normally attacking and looting cargo ships and running the stolen goods into countries where they would have had to pay customs duty had they been legally imported.

"Seems to be a big racket," observed Mallard. Bollard agreed. They had never come across anything like this before.

Several ships were mentioned as possible targets and the sailors made mental notes of their names and sailing times.

When the meeting came to an end, they were taken round to the back courtyard and the Count's study. His greeting was brief.

"Maps," he said, "what's the news on maps?"

Bollard and Mallard began to lay the false trail.

"Yes," Bollard replied, "we've seen the most up-to-date clue. One of the maps is on Comino. Exact location not yet known but they're working on it."

Mallard said, "It would be a nice addition to the one you already have."

Count Cannaregio looked startled. "How did you know there was a map here?" he asked.

"Oh, Wiglington and Wenks have known that for ages," replied Mallard, "in the dungeon room, isn't it?"

"We shall have it moved to a place of safety immediately," muttered the Count obviously flustered at this revelation.

One of his henchmen said something quietly to him. He eyed the sailors suspiciously.

"Do you know more than you are telling us?" he asked.

"That depends," replied Bollard, "we haven't seen any of the money yet."

"I'll give you some to be going on with," said the Count, signalling to his assistant to bring some money across from the safe, "here's a hundred lira for your trouble."

Bollard took the money, flipped through it as though counting it, and put it firmly back on the Count's desk. "It's not enough," he said blankly.

The Count got angry and started banging the table. Bollard and Mallard took no notice.

"I'll make it very painful for you if you don't tell me more," shouted the Count.

"Go ahead," replied Bollard, "and see what good that will do you. Firstly, we shan't be able to get any more information while we are in your prison. Secondly, the Navy will soon realise what has happened. Then you will have their might to contend with. Besides," he concluded, "once we have been under your control do you think they would ever let us know anything of importance again?"

"I agree," chimed in Mallard, wanting to help but not knowing quite how.

"Well, I haven't got any more money up here," said the Count, "so you'll have to go downstairs with my men and they will give you some from the vault. Make sure that you get back to me as soon as you have more information," he ordered.

On the way down to the vault Bollard and Mallard struck up a conversation with the men who were accompanying them. They learnt that the men did not like the Count at all. His smuggling activities had, they implied, got very out of hand. Greed had become his middle name and he was always trying to increase his share of the takings at his gang's expense. Bollard and Mallard sensed mutiny among the ranks.

They took another three hundred lira and went on their way satisfied that they had successfully laid a false trail and given Wiglington and Wenks more time to find their heritage.

CHAPTER 9

IL PALAZZO DEI LUPI

Back at the submarine Bollard and Mallard's story opened up the possibility for Wiglington and Wenks that it might not be so difficult to lay their hands on the next of Carto Wiglington's maps.

The raid on the Palazzo dei Lupi was planned with great care. The Commander was, by now, completely committed to obtaining the map, as opposed to merely protecting Wiglington and Wenks which had been his first charge. They all sat round the mess table munching pastizzi, a delicious Maltese cheese puff, and drinking the local cappuccino.

"I must warn you," Fruba predicted gloomily, "that I heard CorporalBat and his followers talking about the Palazzo. Of course, at the time I didn't know anything about it, nor where it was. But now I hear the name I realise that that is the place they were discussing. My guess is that they will be on the alert for any attack that you might make."

"Yes, yes," said Wiglington trying to minimise the effect of Fruba's prognostications, "we expect that at the very least. Did they give you any indication at all of the layout of the Palazzo or how to reach the dungeon. That's where we're heading for."

"We could always call the police," interjected the Commander, "after all, smuggling is a criminal offence."

"Yes," replied Mr Ruthless, "but we don't have any proof at present, just Bollard and Mallard's word for it. While we believe them, the police might not. No," he continued, "I think we have to go it alone this time and if we find evidence of smuggling, then we can place the matter in the hands of the authorities."

The local Festa *coincided with Wiglington and Wenks' raid on the Palazzo.*

There were a few moonless nights ahead. That, they agreed, would be the ideal time to attack. Preparations were made. They would all travel in the submarine to the nearest point.

Malta is an island of festivals — *Festas*, as they are known locally. They mark the celebration of the Patron Saint's day of different churches and with the large number of churches in Malta there are a lot of *Festas*. The central feature of a *Festa* is the procession which is headed by a group carrying the statue of the saint in whose honour the celebration is taking place. Their next most noticeable characteristic is the display of fireworks. These are not just a few mild bangs with showers of sparks. They are full-blooded, loud explosions which make your ordinary firework seem like a damp squib.

The local *Festa* coincided with Wiglington and Wenks' raid on the Palazzo. All they and the Commander had had in mind was a quiet infiltration, a quick dash to the dungeon and a fast getaway with the Carto Wiglington map.

It didn't turn out quite like that.

The Ratbag had been called on to position itself near the Palazzo as a means of escape for them and the map, should it be necessary to evacuate the area quickly. Its flight had been noticed by CorporalBat who put out a full alert.

Wiglington and Wenks and their supporters approached the building just as the *Festa* got underway. The first they heard was an enormous bang, louder than any thunder. Everyone jumped.

"Good Lord," said Wiglington, "they've brought in the artillery. Are the whole of Europe's defence forces here to combat our little onslaught?"

The bright lights of the fireworks answered his question. They proceeded to the Palazzo and slunk in through a side door Bollard had noticed on his previous visit.

Overhead, CorporalBat's troops were having to cope with a new and unexpected hazard. They had never come across fireworks before and they assumed that what they had flown into was the Royal Navy's answer to batdroppings. They were flying, of course, at standard Fruit Bat height which happens to be the same as fireworks height. All around them the shells, as they thought, were exploding, pouring fire onto them. They dodged and flew this way and that to avoid the flack but there were several casualties among them. Mostly singed wings, deafness and some blindness, but damaging and debilitating nevertheless.

Everyone stops for a *Festa* and the inhabitants of the Palazzo were no exception. They laid aside whatever they were doing to go onto one of the two towers to watch the spectacle. Any sound that Wiglington and Wenks' group might have made was drowned by the din and the display was so ferocious that the spectators from the Palazzo did not even notice CorporalBat and his cronies flying for their lives.

The route to the dungeon was easy. Bollard feared that the map might have been moved after the Count's instructions. But it was there all right. They had no difficulty in extracting it from the safe in which it was kept and they made their exit unnoticed.

It was a deep shock for Count Cannaregio when he discovered the next day that his precious map was gone. He was not, at the best of times, a good-tempered man. Now he was positively livid. He ranted at his incompetent subordinates and cursed and swore at Wiglington and Wenks whom he suspected had stolen the map.

Meanwhile the Genius had come to HMS Repeller to look at the map snatched from the Palazzo. It was certainly a fine specimen and showed the whole of the island in some detail. Landmarks like the Blue Grotto and the cliffs, now known as the Dingli cliffs, were clearly visible.

While studying it the Genius noticed a small square in very faint lines drawn round the Grand Harbour. Down one side of it was written 'three storeys underground'.

"That is definitely a clue," he said, "and my guess is that it refers to an ancient building. The Hypogeum is the only underground building I know in Malta which is three storeys high. I wonder if the Huntergrunden have worked out what it means. In any case there is no time to be lost in seeking it."

The Hypogeum is an ancient temple constructed some four to five thousand years ago. It has to be carefully preserved and to help with this it is open only for three quarters of an hour at a time. Then it is 'rested' for three quarters of an hour. The Genius was able to arrange for Wiglington and Wenks to visit during a rest period so that they wouldn't attract attention. The curator was on hand to greet them.

"I've heard all about Carto Wiglington and I can tell you that we do have a map in the vault here. It's a rather specialised map, showing the Grand Harbour, before it was built up of course. Unique. At least I haven't seen aything like it."

They pored over the map in the curator's office, admiring the detail of the coastline around the natural harbour of Valletta. They also scoured it carefully for signs of a clue about any other maps in Malta.

"Look," squeaked Wenks, the first to spot the lead, "there's an arrow at the west side of the map pointing to a word. What does it say?"

"Gaudisium," replied the Genius, "that means joy and it is the Roman word for Gozo."

"And what do those hands alongside the word mean? They look as though they are being held under running water, don't they?"

"The island is full of baths of various kinds according to the map," replied Wiglington, "they must have been very clean with all that washing."

"Well," answered the Genius, "there's an old wash house at Fontana, just outside Victoria and it might be where Carto decided to lodge his map of the island. We'd better go and look."

It was on their way back to the submarine that things started to go wrong. First, the car in which they were travelling broke down.

"Dust," diagnosed Wiglington, who actually knew very little about cars, "almost certainly dust. Sir Oliver Twit was right, dust is devastating."

Then, just as it looked as if the car was going to start again, Count Cannaregio appeared at the head of a column of wolves and vagabonds. The wolves looked very ferocious, their teeth bared and deep, guttural growls coming from their throats. The vagabonds were threatening with sticks and shouting abuse at Wiglington and his colleagues.

Count Cannaregio appeared at the head of a column of wolves and vagabonds.

At that moment, also, the Ratbag appeared overhead as if the Fruit Bat flyers had instinctively sensed that they were needed.

And, to crown it all, CorporalBat came on the scene. He and his cronies looked considerably the worse for wear. One had his head bandaged. Another was wearing an eye patch which made him look like a pirate. A third sported crutches along his wings.

The battle that followed was more like a game of hide and seek than a fight.

Count Cannaregio's pack was not the best organised. Nor were they particularly brave. Years of smuggling had made them undisciplined and sloppy. They were overfed and underexercised. It was very much to the advantage of their opponents.

"Take the map and fly straight back to the submarine," ordered the Commander, taking charge, "we'll meet you there as soon as we've dealt with this lot."

The Ratbag landed and Wiglington and Wenks jumped in, clutching the map. In no time at all they were airborne and on their way to Valletta. Once there they sent support troops to help the Commander and their other colleagues. It turned out that it was support that they badly needed to win the battle that ensued. In the end the wolves and vagabonds were beaten back. CorporalBat and his motley troop retreated. The sailors, Mr Ruthless and RatGuard returned to base.

Because of the urgency of the mission, the Genius agreed to stay on board for the journey over to Gozo. He knew the island well and could direct them to the Knight's wash house at Fontana, hopefully before the Huntergrunden got wind of it.

Finding the next map and getting it back to the submarine was easy by comparison with what they had been through before. The Huntergrunden seemed to have retired in disarray following the battle. They didn't appear nor were CorporalBat and his friends anywhere to be seen.

Wiglington and Wenks were delighted with Gozo. The charming little island was looking its best with colourful flowers along the streets and roads and an atmosphere quite different from Malta. By comparison Gozo was sleepy, giving the impression a leisurely and of gracious life style in which time did not rule every waking minute.

The Knight's wash house was a ruin but promised to be a fruitful one. There was a very old spout pouring water from a spring. The Genius examined it carefully. Almost all water spouts have a cistern behind them and that means a cavern. Just the place to hide valuables.

The Knight's wash house was a ruin but promised to be a fruitful one.

Chiamassie was Marco Polo's name for Temasek.

This water spout was no different. The tile behind and above the gargoyle presenting his sparkling water so graphically was easily removed to reveal the wooden scroll case containing the map.

It was only after the discovery that there was a flurry of excitement. Predictably, the map was of Gozo and the tiny adjacent island of Comino. But in the bottom right-hand corner of it was a small emblem. It was a lion and the word Chiamassie. They all puzzled over that.

It was the Genius who interpreted it for them. Chiamassie was Marco Polo's name for Temasek, he explained, which itself was the early name for Singapore. The lion was a creature associated with the country by mistake. When it was originally founded the symbol had been that of a tiger. Someone had mistaken it for a lion and so the symbol had been adopted.

Clearly the map they were examining was not of Singapore. The message must be that further maps were to be found there. If that was the case they were in possession of valuable information which presumably the opposition didn't have. They should make the most of it while it was still exclusively theirs, said the Genius.

"Sir Ordy will be ecstatic with the haul this time," said the Genius. He promised to see that the Maltese maps were released and to take them personally to England and deposit them with Sir Ordy while Wiglington and Wenks went on to Singapore.

The Navy had discharged its duty by safeguarding them in Malta. Mr Ruthless felt he had to get back to the office and attend to the growing pile of work waiting for him.

The journey to Singapore was too far for the Ratbag to accomplish in a reasonable time. In order to maintain their head start over the Huntergrunden and CorporalBat, they decided that Wiglington and Wenks should fly to Singapore via Athens. Miss Protectorat would be sent for, to meet up with them on their arrival. Fruba and the Batpack would also meet them there.

Wenks shed a little tear when it came time to say good-bye but cheered up when Wiglington told everyone that they expected they would return one day to the island in the sun.

CHAPTER 10

BRIBERY!

There can be few countries more different than Malta and Singapore. The former has seven thousand years of history. The latter is a modern City-State which has grown largely since the end of the Second World War and most notably in the last thirty years.

Malta is in the Mediterranean with its long, hot, dry, sleepy summers and stormy winters. Singapore is at the hub of Southeast Asia, almost on the equator. There are no seasons except, perhaps, that certain parts of the year are wetter than others. The temperature is constant the year round. And Asia, traditionally, is bustling and busy.

Arriving by plane in Singapore is an experience even for seasoned travellers like Wiglington and Wenks. Changi Airport must be the most efficient in the world. Apart from its primary function of servicing air passengers, it is a shopping and restaurant paradise whether you are flying or not.

But Wiglington and Wenks were not stopping to shop or eat on their way through the airport. They had had a long flight from Malta via Athens and they were tired. They had slept a good deal on the plane but there was a six-hour time change between the two countries and they were suffering from the first real jet-lag they had ever experienced. Jet-lag is when your body thinks the time is what it is in the last country you were in, rather than what it is in the country in which you have just arrived. It can take you up to a week to adjust to the new one.

It had been a very different journey from the one they had made in HMS Repeller. The heavy guard had gone and they were accompanied only by RatGuard. Admittedly, Major Consideration had arranged special clearance at the Malta, Athens and Singapore airports, so they did not have to go through the usual Immigration and Customs channels. Fruba, too, would be joining them once he had completed the long flight. However, they were obviously more exposed than they had been while living in the submarine.

"Look at how green everything is," observed Wenks as they drove into the city, "there must be a lot of rain here for the trees and shrubs to flourish so well."

Wiglington agreed. "Big downpour almost every day," he replied, "keeps the place clean as well as green. It also makes it very damp." They had noticed the humidity as soon as they stepped outside the airport and before they had climbed into the air-conditioned car.

Arriving by plane in Singapore is an experience even for seasoned travellers like Wiglington and Wenks.

"We're going to feel a little lost without the Genius to help us, aren't we?" continued Wenks.

"Yes," answered Wiglington, "and we don't have much of a clue as to where the map in Singapore may be hidden. The Genius suggested that we talk to the people at the museum first. They may know."

Their hotel was magnificent. Even though they had had the special stateroom on HMS Repeller it didn't compare with this. They had a big bowl of fruit from the Manager with a little card

"Look at how green everything is," observed Wenks as they drove into the city, "there must be lots of rain here for the trees and shrubs to flourish so well."

welcoming them. There were flowers from well-wishers who had heard of their exploits. There was an invitation to an entertainment extravaganza in the hotel gardens one evening. And there were menus galore from the many restaurants, each producing a different style of cooking.

Their fame had reached Singapore ahead of them and there were several people who wanted to meet them. The phone started to ring as soon as they arrived. RatGuard was taking messages and making appointments for them. It looked as though they were going to be busy.

"How very kind people are," observed Wenks, "who'd have thought we were so well-know?" I guess it's all due to Carto Wiglington. We certainly seem to be better known here than anywhere else."

They spent the next few days sightseeing while waiting for Fruba and the Batpack to arrive. Miss Protectorat who arrived shortly after they did enjoyed the excursion to the Botanical

Gardens best. They were also most impressed with their ride on the country's brand new MRT (Mass Rapid Transport) or subway system, and with their visit to the beautifully restored Raffles Hotel.

They wined and dined with their new-found Singaporean friends who were extremely generous. They tucked into delicious satay and fish head curry which singed their palates. They feasted on goreng pisang (banana fritters) and mouth-watering poh-piah (spring rolls).

The best meal they had was at Mabel's Table. Aunty Mabel, as she was fondly known, served them an eight-course, home-cooked Nonya-style meal, a special blend of Malay and Chinese cooking. They especially enjoyed the gula melaka, a sweet pudding with coconut milk that completed the meal.

Many of their Singaporean friends were keen to take them shopping which, they teased, would go a long way to contribute to the growth of the national economy. Wiglington breathed a sigh of relief when Wenks declined an offer to buy a cultured pearl necklace but settled instead for some silk material.

They were in this jolly mood when Fruba and his Batpack caught up with them.

They had also by this time worked their way through all the invitations to one from a Mr Tan who said that he was a local businessman and would welcome the opportunity to show them the non-tourist, rural parts of Singapore. It seemed like an ideal thing to do after their extensive tour of the city.

The day was hot and sunny, like most days in Singapore. Wiglington and Wenks were collected by Mr Tan at the appointed time in a brand new Mercedes Benz and taken with two of his colleagues to Ponggol. There they enjoyed a delicious lunch of chilli crabs which were spicy hot and required a lot of work with the paws.

After lunch Mr Tan invited them to join him for a boat ride to a nearby island. They welcomed a trip on the water and were soon on board a fast motor launch heading across the sea to their destination. In the distance they saw what looked like Fruba flying towards them but Mr Tan said it was a fish eagle. At that range they couldn't tell.

"Where exactly are we going?" asked Wiglington, somewhat alarmed at the speed with which they had departed. He was glad RatGuard and Miss Protectorat were with them.

"To an island called Pulau Ubin," replied Mr Tan, "it is less built up than Singapore and much more rustic. You will be able to see what Singapore is like off the beaten track."

Wiglington and Wenks were pleased with the prospect of seeing a part of Singapore that tourists do not often get the opportunity to explore.

After a short journey the launch came to rest alongside a little jetty and Mr Tan led the way ashore. The tiny island is very different from Singapore. Where Singapore has tall concrete blocks, Pulau Ubin has rambling villages of tin and palm-thatched or attap-roofed wooden houses. The roads are dirt tracks, many leading to scrub land and forest.

They were taken along one of the dirt tracks, heading towards the forest where Mr Tan said that they would be shown some special species of plants and flora that were unique to this part of the world.

It was very hot and mosquitoes were buzzing round them. They hadn't come across any mosquitoes in Singapore city and were beginning to regret having agreed to undertake the journey, when they came upon a tin-roofed shack in a clearing.

They heard low snarls and growls and on turning to face them, the party found itself surrounded by a pack of wolves. They were not unlike the ones they had seen in Malta, but better fed and groomed.

Two of the wolves sprang on poor RatGuard and Miss Protectorat and gripped them in their jaws. RatGuard and Miss Protectorat shrieked with pain and fear and so did Wiglington and Wenks whose paws were being twisted by Mr Tan.

Mr Tan shoved Wiglington and Wenks into the shack. His friends and the wolves squeezed in.

One of the wolves was bigger than the rest. He spoke first.

They heard low snarls and growls and on turning to face them, the party found itself surrounded by a pack of wolves.

"I am Warrior Wolf and we are the Sea Wolf Council," he said in a deep voice, "we want Carto Wiglington's maps and are prepared to make you a generous offer. We will deposit a sum of twenty thousand rollers for each map that you find and hand over to us. We are a much more powerful force than the Fruit Bats. If you agree to let us have the maps, we shall protect you from the Fruit Bats and use our extensive resources to help you in your search. You will not find a more generous offer than this, I guarantee," he ended.

A roller is worth about the same as a dollar.

"The maps are not for sale." said Wiglington. "They represent a priceless heritage and we want them exhibited in museums around the world for all to see. That way we can increase the interest in cartography and encourage people to learn more geography and history. We also want them to be more conscious of the environment. Besides, by exhibiting the maps we shall acquire money to award scholarships for the study of these things."

"What a speech!" mocked Warrior Wolf. "Who are you kidding? Do you expect me to believe that you cannot be bought? There is always a price. Just name yours. How about thirty thousand per map?"

Wiglington was feeling highly insulted and very indignant. Before he could reply, they heard a terrific banging on the tin roof and hideous, high pitched, screeching sounds. The room was filled with the odour of batdroppings falling through the holes in the roof.

In the twinkle of an eye, several bats had found their way into the shack and were pelting the wolves and Mr Tan.

"Eek!" screamed one of the wolves, "Can't stand bats. They get in the fur and cause chaos." He dived for cover under a small table in the corner of the shack.

"Ouch! My eyes! I'm blinded. I can't see," howled the wolf who was gripping Miss Protectorat in his jaws, and promptly dropped her.

She gave the wolf who was holding RatGuard a karate chop on the paw, forcing him to drop RatGuard and yelp in pain. RatGuard and Miss Protectorat pushed Mr Tan onto the floor and grabbed Wiglington and Wenks, whisking them out of the shack through a hole in a wall.

The four of them raced through the undergrowth along the dirt track leading to the jetty, leaving the pandemonium behind them. Fruba and his Fruit Bats kept up the attack, swooping down from the sky and into the shed where the wolves' cries of "Get away!" and "No, not my best fur" and "Ouch, stop biting" could be heard together with yelps of pain whenever the Fruit Bats were nipped by the wolves. The fierce battle raged on.

After what seemed like hours, but was, in reality, just a few minutes, Wiglington and Wenks spotted the boat and jumped on board. It was then that they realised that the boat wouldn't start without its key. The key, they assumed, was still with Mr Tan.

RatGuard searched the lockers and found several lengths of rope. Miss Protectorat cottoned on to what he was doing. She let out a piercing and most unladylike whistle to attract Fruba's attention. He understood at once what was needed and called his Fruit Bats off the attack and down to the boat.

By the time they reached it the ends of the ropes were attached to the bow. Each Fruit Bat grasped one rope in his claws and they flew off, pulling the launch away from the landing stage, out into the sea.

As they looked back, Wiglington and Wenks saw the figures of Mr Tan and his friends standing on the jetty shaking their fists. Behind them the wolves were assembling sheepishly.

Back at their hotel RatGuard rang the police who told him that they had been searching for Mr Tan for some time. He was wanted in connection with a smuggling ring which was operating between Singapore and one of the neighbouring countries.

The Huntergrunden, if they were caught, would be charged with attempted kidnapping and extradited for trial by the European Court.

"Thank goodness you turned up when you did," said Wenks to Fruba, "I hate to think what would have happened if you hadn't."

Fruba was pleased with himself. His information network was being active and efficient. Some time back he had wondered if he

Each Fruit Bat grasped one rope in his claws and they flew off . . . .

was losing control. Now he had demonstrated that he was very much in charge. Of everyone, it was Wenks who was most grateful to him. He could see that she was beginning to like and trust him.

"My information is," he began, "that the Huntergrunden lost a lot of face when you escaped in Malta and they are determined to show their strength. Warrior Wolf was assigned the task of getting the maps from you by hook or by crook. He is under tremendous pressure to succeed, as failure means he will lose the position of head of the Huntergrunden."

"Warrior Wolf has another problem, though," continued Fruba, pleased that he was able to pass on so much information, "he thinks Mr Tan is on his side. Mr Tan, however, wants the maps for himself and his gang of Flying Foxes. They were co-operating with Warrior Wolf and the pack because they thought that would be the quickest way to achieve their goal. The Flying Foxes are rivals of the Fruit Bats. They are meaner, too. Once they have located the treasure they will drive Warrior Wolf and his cronies out of Singapore. Asian gangs like the Flying Foxes do not care for intrusion into their territories."

"How are we going to out-smart Warrior Wolf and now, Mr Tan and the Flying Foxes?" asked Wiglington. "We don't even know the location of the next map ourselves, nor where to start looking for it. The last thing we need are two forces working against us in Singapore."

It sounded difficult.

Another well-wisher, a Mr Lee, had invited them to a Chinese dinner at a little restaurant in New Bridge Road.

"What I suggest we do," continued Fruba now feeling comfortably in command of the situation, "is that we go out and have a jolly good meal tonight. The Singaporeans regard that as an excellent preliminary to solving problems and I agree with them. First thing in the morning we will visit the man at the museum and see what he can tell us. By that time I shall have assembled the biggest force of Fruit Bats Southeast Asia has ever seen. If that isn't some protection against the Huntergrunden and Flying Foxes, I'll eat my Bathat," (A Bathat is to Fruit Bats what a hat is to humans, only Fruit Bats actually eat their Bathats when they say they will. Humans don't.)

"Besides," he added, "the police may have Mr Tan and the Huntergrunden in hand by now so that only leaves us the Flying Foxes, who will be waiting for Mr Tan's signal."

Their meal that evening was delicious. Another well-wisher, a Mr Lee, had invited them to a Chinese dinner at a little restaurant in New Bridge Road. Apparently you weren't allowed to sing there. Anyway there was a big notice over the door which said Ban Sing or something like it. But Wiglington and Wenks wanted to eat not to sing so they didn't mind. By the time they got to bed they were two happily full Water Rats glowing with the inner peace of having feasted on delectable sharks fin soup and braised goose meat.

They were fast asleep when the note was pushed underneath their door.

CHAPTER 11

THE WISE ONE

Wenks noticed it first, lying on the carpet just inside their bedroom door. It was written in a flowery script and it said "Please join us to celebrate the forthcoming Festival of Lights. See the fire walking ceremony. You will also learn about your maps there."

Naturally, after the invitation they had had to lunch they were very wary of any suggestions about where they should go, especially from anonymous sources. However, after discussing the matter with RatGuard and Miss Protectorat, and after establishing that there would be a big squadron of Fruit Bats in attendance, they concluded that a place where there were lots of people around could hardly be risky. They were all intrigued with the idea of watching a fire walking ceremony that precedes the celebration of Deepavali, an important feast in the Hindu calendar. So they decided to attend.

Before then, however, there was the museum to explore.

The man at the museum had been informed about their visit and he was expecting them. He welcomed them with tea, not the sort they were used to in England but strong, bitter tea to wake you up and keep your attention focused.

"I've read quite a lot about Carto Wiglington and his maps and, of course, your map rescue attempt is now widely known in cartographic and archivist circles," he said after introducing himself as Dr Saw. "I'm not very knowledgeable about maps but I know a little and I have learnt that some of Carto's maps were indeed brought to Singapore, but a long time after his death. By his great, great grandson, it would appear. The story," he continued, warming to his theme, "was that Carto knew of Singapore but never visited it himself. He decided however that it would be a good place to keep some of the maps he was drawing of the southern hemisphere so he left a message somewhere that they should be brought here."

He paused.

"Where did this message appear?" asked Wiglington.

"That we don't know. Probably on a map drawn before he came south. It seems that he may have thought Singapore was central and he would certainly return to Europe this way. As you know, he was swept out to sea in a storm off the Great Barrier Reef so sadly he never did return. But he left us a wonderful legacy of his work, didn't he?"

Wiglington and Wenks nodded in agreement.

"We think we've seen the message to which you refer," intervened Wenks, "it appeared on a map we found in Gozo, a small island off the coast of Malta. It mentioned Chiamassie and the Genius said that was the old word for Temasek, the original name of Singapore."

Dr Saw smiled and said that was, indeed, the case.

"Did this clue in Gozo give you any idea where you might find the map or maps in Singapore?" he asked.

"No," replied Wiglington, "in fact, nobody has a clue. So I have come to you as the man most likely to be able to give us a lead."

"Oh dear," sighed Dr Saw, "I hope I'm not going to let you down. Are there no other clues at all?" he asked.

Wiglington told him about the note they had received in their hotel room but he didn't mention the Huntergrunden and Mr Tan. He felt rather foolish about that episode.

Dr Saw couldn't tell them anything immediately but promised to look into the matter. He suggested that they might like to see some of the sights of Singapore and arranged for one of his colleagues to take them on a cable car ride to Sentosa.

* * * * * * * * * * * *

Warrior Wolf was thoroughly fed up. He had lost out to Wiglington and Wenks in Malta, due largely to the indiscipline of his colleagues there. Then there had been the fiasco at Pulau Ubin where they narrowly escaped arrest by the police. Not only had Warrior Wolf lost his dignity but Mr Tan had lost his boat. Worse, the authorities were now aware of the Huntergrunden's presence which would make the job of getting hold of the map that much more difficult. What was worse was that he expected the highly efficient police force to alert Interpol about their presence and this was bound to make Head Office nervous.

He summoned his colleagues and gave them a strict talking to.

"This cannot go on any longer," he warned, glaring at the assembled pack, "we have another chance to wrest the maps from the Rats tomorrow. They have obviously decided to play tough and not accept our generous proposal of money and help. I am declaring war on them now. My sources tell me that Wiglington and Wenks will be going to the Festival of Lights celebrations tonight and I suspect it is to find out where their maps are hidden. If we track them from the hotel we shall see who they talk to and where they go. With any luck we should be able to find the next map."

Warrior Wolf looked at the motley group in front of him. They were bored. Some were scratching, finding the heat unpleasant and inclined to give them a rash. Others were yawning, a few muttering to each other. They needed waking up.

"It has been my intention for some time to consider appointing a deputy, someone who can look after things when I am away," he paused, "and someone who can possibly take over from me when I retire."

The words had an electrifying effect. Wolves are very competitive, especially when it comes to food or power. They sat up straight, trying to appear taller than those around them so that they would be noticed. The muttering and scratching stopped.

"I should like to volunteer," said Willie Wolf, one of the smaller members, "to lead the pack into Little India for the festival."

"Very kind of you," replied Warrior Wolf, "but we shan't be making that sort of an entrance. No, I want you all to act like dogs and mingle among the crowd. You will be issued special walkie-talkie sets that come in the form of dog collars that will enable you to keep in touch with me. When you learn anything of importance you will let me know."

He went on to give them a detailed briefing.

****

Mr Tan was holding a similar meeting in a warehouse near the World Trade Centre. Only his meeting was attended by the Flying Foxes. They were not in need of any of the sort of motivation Warrior Wolf had been handing out. The enemy, as far as the Flying Foxes were concerned, was the Huntergrunden. They were invading their territory and had to be seen off.

The Flying Foxes knew the area well even though they had never attended the Festival of Lights. They would have no difficulty in finding their way around the crowd and if the wolves put in an appearance they would attack immediately.

****

Wiglington and Wenks were a little nervous about going to the Festival of Lights celebrations. RatGuard and Miss Protectorat reassured them that they would be well looked after. They had seen spectacular sights in their travels but this was something different. Little India was ablaze with lights and there were hundreds of people milling around a fair. The air was perfumed by the sweet scent of flowers and incense, and the shops were festively decorated. Many of the restaurants and coffee shops displayed a wide array of tempting sweets and delicacies. The temples were crowded and thousands and thousands of candles were alight, casting dancing shadows against the walls.

Wiglington and Wenks looked around to see if anyone was searching for them. They had no idea how whoever it was was going to make contact. There were so many people that it seemed

Little India was ablaze with lights and there were hundreds of people milling around.

quite likely they would never reach the anonymous sender of the note.

RatGuard, too, and Miss Protectorat looked this way and that studying the faces of the worshippers for any trace of interest. But the people were concentrating on getting ready for the procession and for the most part were totally involved in prayer.

As they were walking slowly towards a building near the temple which they hoped would give them a good view when the procession started, someone tapped Wiglington on the arm. Wiglington swung round to see a smiling Indian man beckoning him towards a side street off the main path of the proceedings. They all followed the man because he had an honest face and, sure enough, when they had got some distance from the noise he began to speak to them.

"May I please ask if you are Wiglington and Wenks?" he asked, smiling all the time.

"Yes," replied Wiglington, "do you have some information for us?"

"I am to tell you that you must go to a Guru not far from here. Mr Rajagopal is one of the wisest men in Singapore. He will guide you to your maps."

At that moment two dogs standing nearby leant close to Wiglington, trying to hear what the man was saying. Wiglington caught a whiff of their breath and recognised it immediately as the same as that which he had smelled in the tin shed on Pulau Ubin. They were undoubtedly wolves and not dogs.

Wiglington was about to take the law into his own hands when there was a *whooshing* of wings overhead. It sounded as though a huge flock of birds was descending. He looked up. There was what looked like a group of Fruit Bats moving in on them. They didn't look like Fruba or his mob, though.

It was soon obvious that these were the Flying Foxes. Wiglington pulled Wenks into a doorway for shelter and they watched as the intruders set about attacking the two wolves.

The attack didn't last long. The lights of Little India were too bright for the Flying Foxes and almost as quickly as they had appeared they were gone and the two wolves had slunk off into the crowd.

Following their guide they set off quickly through back streets and down little alleys until they came to a small shop-house in Buffalo Road. Their guide took them upstairs and they entered a small, dark room which had a strong smell of incense.

Sitting on the floor, cross-legged was a very old man with a turban. He had a long white beard. He motioned Wiglington and Wenks to sit down on a mat on the floor.

For a while the old man sat in silence and their guide who had brought them indicated that they should not interrupt his thoughts. Finally he spoke.

"I am Rajagopal," he said to Wiglington, "you are Wiging?"

"Not quite," said Wiglington, pronouncing his name properly and introducing Wenks.

"Certainly," replied Mr Rajagopal, continuing, "you are descended from a very famous map maker, His Excellency Mr Carto Wiglington, is it not?"

Wiglington nodded.

"I have been waiting for you for a very long time. We are most privileged to have some of His Excellency's maps here in Singapore," he paused and studied Wiglington and Wenks to see what their reactions were. "I have a vision of where you may find the maps but first I must look into the future and tell you what to expect." He shut his eyes and meditated for a while. Then he turned to Wenks.

"Wenks will have a long and happy life. A tall, dark, slightly older Water Rat will spend much time with her. She will travel a great deal and will be very successful in her chosen career." Wenks gave him a big smile.

"Wiglington," he continued, "will be making long journeys for many years to come. His mission is to collect his ancestor's maps and he will have many obstacles to overcome. But he will triumph in the end if he perseveres. He will never be rich but he will have a most interesting life and win the acclaim of his fellow Water Rats. He will be famous in many parts of the world."

"I have a vision of where you may find the maps . . . ."

Wiglington glowed with pride at the forecast.

Wenks began to get impatient. "Where can we locate the Carto Wiglington maps, please?" she asked in an effort to hurry things along.

"They are to be found where orchids rest in Loyang," replied Mr Rajagopal, "you will find what you seek. I can tell you no more than that," he said.

Wiglington and Wenks thanked Mr Rajagopal and with a little wave of his hand, he dismissed them.

As they left the shop-house they puzzled over the clue "where orchids rest" and so did not notice several shadowy figures following them down Buffalo Road.

CHAPTER 12

ORCHIDS LAST FOREVER

When they got back to their hotel, Wiglington and Wenks found a message from an Inspector Salleh bin Ismail requesting that they meet first thing in the morning.

Following a breakfast of Chinese porridge, called Congee, which they found delicious, they met up with RatGuard, Miss Protectorat, Fruba and the Inspector who told them that the Huntergrunden and Mr Tan were still at large, having escaped from Pulau Ubin after a dramatic chase by the Marine Police.

The Inspector warned Wiglington and Wenks to keep a sharp look out for the Huntergrunden and Mr Tan who, he said, headed a gang of Flying Foxes. RatGuard and Miss Protectorat thanked the Inspector for the information and said that they would continue to keep Rat Alert so that Wiglington and Wenks would be well protected.

"I wonder if you can help us with a clue that we were given last night," asked Wenks of the Inspector. "A wise man in Little India suggested that the maps we are looking for may be in a place where orchids rest in Loyang. Where is Loyang and what do you think he meant by orchids resting?"

The Inspector thought for a bit, frowned, then beamed. "I know," he said. "Loyang used to be swamp land years ago. It has been redeveloped and there is now an industrial site where there is a factory that produces gold-plated products including orchids."

"You mean the gold orchids we have seen in shops all over Singapore and in tourist brochures?" asked Wenks.

"Precisely," replied the Inspector. "I suggest that you visit the orchid factory to see if the maps are there."

As soon as the Inspector had gone, the hotel doorman hailed a taxi. He was impressively dressed to resemble a Mongolian Warrior. He told the driver to take them to the orchid factory in Loyang.

The taxi-driver was very law-abiding, travelling quite slowly. Wiglington asked once or twice if it would be possible to speed up but when the driver did so a little bell started to ring to remind him that he was exceeding the speed limit and he had to slow down.

Every now and then Wiglington and Wenks peered out of the back of the taxi. On one occasion when they did so they saw a big black cloud following them, Flying Foxes undoubtedly.

"Looks pretty ominous to me," observed Wiglington. RatGuard and Miss Protectorat were concerned, too.

"They seem a really vicious mob," observed Wenks, which didn't help to cheer anyone up much.

RatGuard decided that it was prudent to alert Fruba to the situation and he did so just before they arrived at the factory.

When they arrived at the factory they asked to see the Manager who was very welcoming and sympathetic to their cause. Wiglington told Mr De Souza about the Carto Wiglington maps. He explained how he had been directed to the factory. He mentioned the clue, "where orchids rest", and warned Mr De Souza of the enemies — the Flying Foxes circling overhead and the Huntergrunden who had not yet arrived but might at any moment.

Intrigued, Mr De Souza showed Wiglington and Wenks the place "where orchids rest", a room filled with the most magnificent array of colourful flowers. There were freshly cut blooms of all sorts of sizes and shapes.

He showed them where selected orchids were dipped in gold to turn them into fashion pieces for the jewellery shops. Wiglington was so taken with the idea that he asked to buy one for Wenks and Mr De Souza promised a special discount which would make it a very good buy.

"Well," said Mr De Souza, "I'm not sure how else to help you. We have certainly not seen any maps around here and I was here when the factory was first being built."

Wiglington asked, "Can we stay and have a closer look at the room where orchids rest before they are dipped in gold? The maps may be in there somewhere."

"By all means," replied Mr De Souza. "Take your time. I shall have to leave you for a short while in any case since I have a meeting. I wish you luck in the search."

Wiglington and Wenks, RatGuard and Miss Protectorat worked out a plan to search the room inch by inch, each beginning from a different corner. It was Miss Protectorat who called out with delight after a few minutes. She had come across a loose tile on the floor under the table on which rested Golden Showers, a delightfully sunny, yellow coloured orchid. She pawed at the tile and pried it loose, disclosing a deep hole, at the bottom of which was a gunny sack made of jute fibres. Miss Protectorat scrambled down the hole to retrieve the sack and when she surfaced, the others crowded round to see what it contained.

Inside the sack they found a sealed, waterproof rubber bag containing four maps, each of which bore Carto Wiglington's famous signature. One of the maps was of Ceylon, now called Sri Lanka. Another two were of Sumatra and Java, both parts of Indonesia today. The fourth was of Siam now known as Thailand. It meant that although Carto Wiglington had never visited Singapore himself he had got extremely close which is, no doubt, why he wanted the maps to be lodged there.

They had been so engrossed in looking for the maps that they had not noticed the commotion outside the factory and in the production room nearby.

The Huntergrunden had realised after the attack in Little India that Mr Tan had betrayed them. They now realised that he and his Flying Foxes were their enemy. They had trailed Wiglington and Wenks back to their hotel and kept vigilant watch. It had paid off as they saw Wiglington and Wenks board the taxi for the factory.

Using their special walkie-talkies, the guard wolves had radioed Warrior Wolf and told him to get the rest of the pack to the orchid factory. Warrior Wolf and his troop surrounded the factory so that no one could get in or out of the premises without their knowledge.

In the meantime, the Flying Foxes had followed the taxi to the factory. Some of them were hovering around outside, hoping to whisk the maps off Wiglington and Wenks should they find them. Others had gained entry into the factory and were looking for their quarry.

It was at this point that a second black cloud appeared on the horizon. Fruba and his Fruit Bats swooped down on the Flying Foxes and engaged in wing-to-wing combat. Claws were extended and the powerful beat of the wings made a noise like the whine of distant sirens.

It was chaos all round with Flying Foxes fighting Fruit Bats and both fighting the wolves.

The Huntergrunden had moved in now, closer to the action. When the Fruit Bats or the Flying Foxes came near the ground they made a grab for them but the flyers were too quick. It was chaos all round with Flying Foxes fighting Fruit Bats and both fighting the wolves.

Batdroppings were falling all over the place and the Flying Foxes saw some swift action by Fruba as he battled with his opponent at close range. Suddenly one of the smaller Flying Foxes found himself in the grip of a Fruit Bat stranglehold. The Fruit Bat almost lost him but managed to hang on. He dived towards what he thought was a vat of water, but it wasn't. It was gold. The Fruit Bat hurled the Flying Fox into the vat and flew off to join his colleagues.

It was about a minute later that the small creature bobbed to the surface of the gold tank. Two of his fellow Flying Foxes dived low to pull him out but it was too late. The Flying Fox had been covered in gold-plate which had set very quickly. He was destined forever to be a Flying Fox Souvenir — the only one of its kind.

This event demoralised the Flying Foxes so much that they beat a hasty retreat, pursued by the Huntergrunden who mistakenly thought they had got hold of something valuable, possibly a map.

Once more the battleground was quiet. Wiglington and Wenks, RatGuard and Miss Protectorat emerged from their room with the maps to a dazed audience. Mr De Souza and his colleagues could not believe what they had just seen and experienced. The Quality Control Supervisor was appalled by the contamination of the vat, muttering darkly that it would be difficult to convince shareholders that gold was lost in a battle among Flying Foxes and Fruit Bats. The factory personnel who were used to producing ornamental gold-plated animals of the Chinese Zodiac could not conceive of a gold-plated Flying Fox.

"That Flying Fox is worth quite a lot of money," said Mr De Souza, concerned at the amount of gold that had been absorbed by the creature.

"All in a good cause," replied Wiglington, with a twinkle in his eye. "We shall keep a look out in town and if we find him on sale we'll say that he belongs to you. Meanwhile," he continued, "I would like to buy a couple of souvenirs from you."

With that, the party proceeded to the Showroom where Wenks selected some jewellery for herself and her friends.

"Now, we have a more serious matter to attend to," said RatGuard, "we need to get the maps to England as soon as possible and it is going to be quite hazardous. There are many places between here and Changi where the Flying Foxes or the Huntergrunden could intercept us. We must plan the safest and quickest route. If Mr De Souza will kindly safeguard the maps for a day or so I shall try to arrange something."

"With pleasure," promised Mr De Souza, "we have a very strong safe here to which only I and my assistant have the combination. The maps will be safe with us."

They moved off, leaving the staff to clean up the batdroppings, keeping them carefully since they make excellent fertiliser.

RatGuard did a splendid job of negotiating. First, he made sure that Singapore Airlines could carry them all to London. As there are daily flights that presented no problem. Then he sought the Inspector's help, explaining to him the difficulties posed by their enemies. After a very helpful meeting it was decided that Wiglington and Wenks would get a police escort to Changi Airport while RatGuard would collect the maps from the orchid factory and make his way separately in an armoured van.

They sent messages to Sir Ordy at the British Museum telling him of the coup and asking for his help with safe transport in England. He faxed back that not only would there be an armoured car at the airport but he would buy them a good lunch at the Mappin Club. They were looking forward to that.

The day of departure began with a downpour. It only lasted an hour but the wind howled and the rain beat down like they had never seen if before.

"This explains why there are so many buildings with porches in Singapore," remarked Wiglington, "so you don't get too wet."

The gale was so strong that it brought down quite a number of branches from the trees. In an hour it was all over and shortly after, the sun came out and it got very hot again.

"All ready for the return journey?" enquired RatGuard as Miss Protectorat helped them to collect the cases together that evening, "We have a little surprise for you."

They stepped outside the hotel and there was a vintage car with an excited crowd standing round admiring it. The driver brought it to the door and they climbed in. The hood was down so the crowd could see Wiglington and Wenks and several people called 'Selamat Jalan' which means goodbye in Malay.

"You will be entirely safe," said RatGuard, "with your police escort and Fruba and his squadron will keep the Flying Foxes and Wolves at bay. See you at the airport," he added.

And with that RatGuard went off to pick up the maps.

What RatGuard had deliberately not told Wiglington and

They stepped outside the hotel and there was a vintage car ....

Wenks was that he hoped that their high visibility would attract so much attention that he could slip away unnoticed.

The ruse worked and both parties arrived at the airport without incident. They were accorded VIWR (Very Important Water Rats) treatment, the equivalent of VIP (Very Important Persons) treatment and found their special departure lounge very much to their liking. Their seats on the big plane were so comfortable that they fell asleep soon after take-off and didn't wake for several hours by which time they were well on the way to England.

Arriving at London Airport at five-thirty in the morning local time, they noticed that it was starting to get distinctly chilly. Autumn was coming to an end and soon the leaves would be turning brown and dropping, heralding the onset of winter.

They were beginning to feel completely relaxed when they were accosted by a couple who leapt out of a side door of the air terminal. These two ruffians gagged them and tied up their paws, chucking them roughly into a deep square metal bin on wheels. They were trundled rapidly down several corridors and out of the building, across an airport road and into a waiting van. CorporalBat was sitting inside.

"At last," he said with a leer, "at last we have captured the Rats with some maps. Search them and take their treasure," he ordered the man who had kidnapped them.

Poor Wiglington and Wenks squirmed while the two performed a rough body search on them. They then turned to the travel bags, ripping them open and spilling the contents onto the floor of the van.

There were several personal items of clothing, reading books and a travel game but no maps.

"Nothing," said the woman.

"Zero," said the man.

"Batdroppings!" exclaimed CorporalBat. "Ungag them. I'll make them tell us where the maps are," he threatened.

"The maps are on the luggage belt," said Wiglington, as soon as the gag was taken off. "You won't be able to find them without our help. They are very well disguised. You will have to take us there yourselves so that we can point them out to you."

They then turned to the travel bags, ripping them open and spilling the contents onto the floor of the van.

After some thought, CorporalBat decided that he had no choice but to set off to the baggage area with Wiglington and Wenks, which wasn't a very bright idea. It didn't occur to him that he should have kept Wenks in the van until Wiglington handed the maps over to him. Nor did he ask himself why Wiglington and Wenks were not escorted by RatGuard.

They all made their way to the Baggage Claim area where CorporalBat was eagerly expecting to lay his claws on the maps.

Meanwhile, RatGuard had smelt a mouse, if you'll pardon the expression, when Wiglington and Wenks did not show up at the Baggage Claim area. He had had the maps placed in a special briefcase chained to his paws and between Miss Protectorat and him, they had ensured throughout the journey that the priceless haul did not leave their side.

RatGuard, realising that something was amiss, dispatched Miss Protectorat with the maps to the British Museum in a taxi. It would attract less attention than the armoured car that Sir Ordy had arranged.

Then he enlisted the help of Airport Security to place some staff at strategic points in the Baggage Claim area.

RatGuard's hunch was right. Wiglington and Wenks had very cleverly hoodwinked CorporalBat into coming to the luggage belt.

He signalled to the security men who moved in quietly and arrested CorporalBat and his cronies. The arrest was done so

Their arrival at the British Museum was spectacular.

quietly and efficiently that the other passengers waiting at the luggage belt didn't even realise what was happening. Neither did CorporalBat until it was too late.

Their arrival at the British Museum was spectacular. Sir Ordy, as usual, was waiting on the steps but so were several of their other friends. Castle had come over from Paris for the occasion. Mr Ruthless was there. Reggie Rat and H Vaulter had shown up and Wiglington and Wenks were deeply honoured to see Petrov and Miss Angela. Perhaps the biggest surprise was Dr Damp, all the way from Istanbul. He had been on a business trip to London and had called on Sir Ordy to find out how the map hunting was going. Dr Damp still had his cold but was now sporting a very smartly embroidered Turkish made handkerchief instead of his flimsy tissues. The Genius was there, too, with the maps from Malta.

Once the maps were safely stored Sir Ordy took them all to the Mappin Club for a good lunch. Later on, he drove Wiglington and Wenks back to Bentley and saw them safely into their home.

It was a full moon that night and after supper Wiglington and Wenks went for a walk round the village. The barricades around their house had been removed and things seemed pretty much back to normal. It was good to breathe the clean air and smell the country scents again.

"No place like home, is there?" asked Wenks.

Wiglington grunted contentedly.

"No place like home, is there?" said Wenks. Wiglington grunted contentedly.

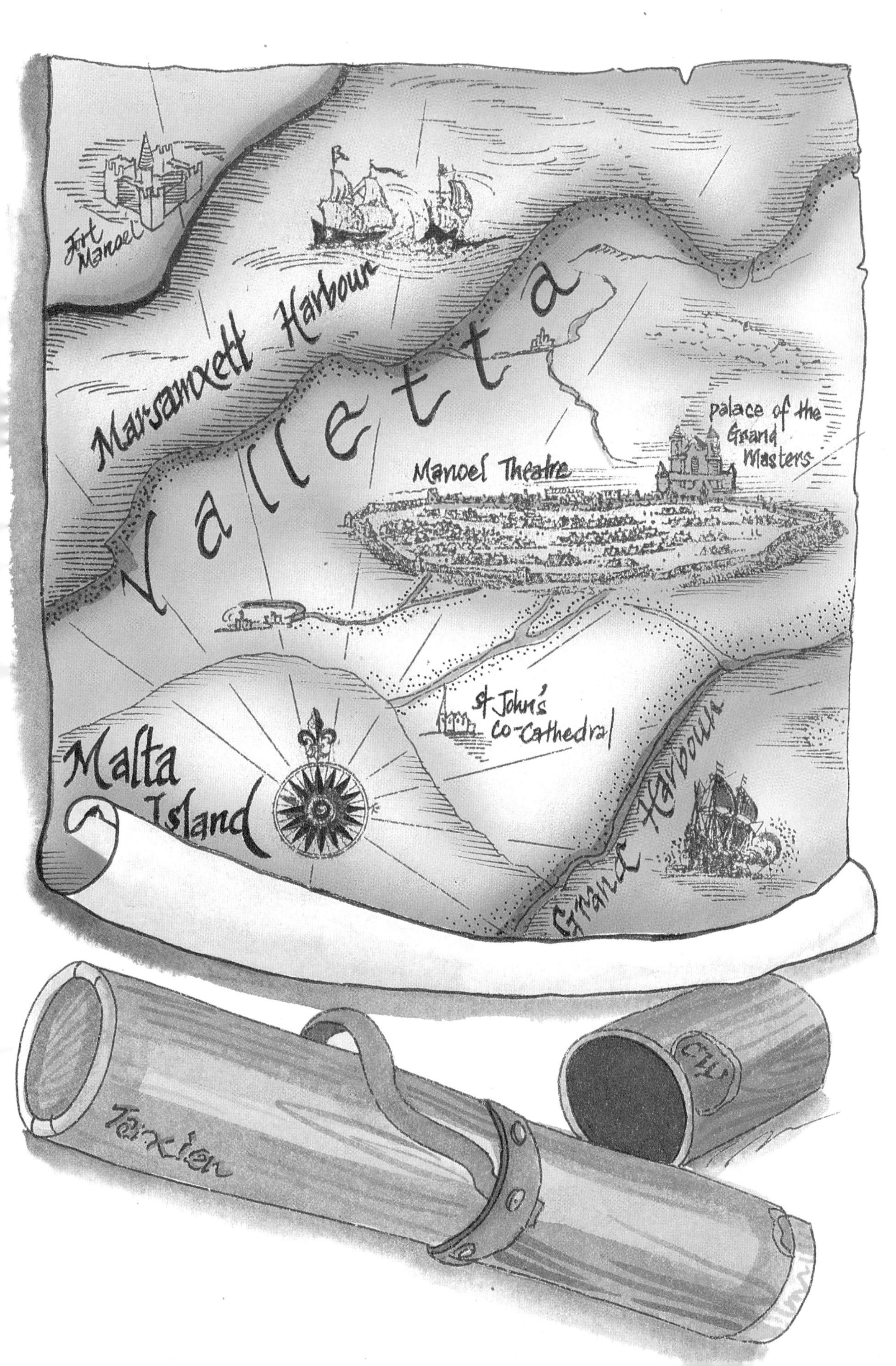
Fort Manoel
Marsamxett Harbour
Valletta
palace of the Grand Masters
Manoel Theatre
St John's Co-Cathedral
Malta Island
Grand Harbour
Taxien
CW